di francis

DEATH ON DARTMOOR

"A thriller from the Doyenne of British Mystery Cat research"

Technical Editor: Richard Freeman
Edited: Corinna Downes
Typeset by Jessica Heard,
Cover and Layout by SPiderKaT for CFZ Communications
Using Microsoft Word 2000, Microsoft Publisher 2000, Adobe Photoshop CS.

First published in Great Britain by CFZ Press

**CFZ Press
Myrtle Cottage
Woolsery
Bideford
North Devon
EX39 5QR**

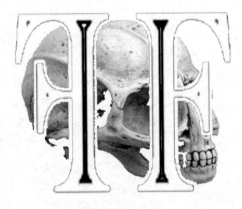

© CFZ MMXII

ISBN: 978-1-905723-97-3

The peaceful beauty of the Devon countryside is threatened when the killings begin. But what or who is responsible for the rising number of victims? A reclusive old poacher, Trapper, could have identified the killer if he hadn't become a victim himself. Stories abound and legends are revived, and the killings continue. The few people who suspect they have the answer are ignored by the authorities. How many have to die before anyone will listen?

CHAPTER 1

Young John Crabb crouched in the undergrowth, hardly daring to breathe, willing his heart to stop thumping so loudly. He took in his breath slowly, deeply, trying to control his lungs. If he didn't, they would hear and find him! He felt he was making enough noise to alert the whole wood, and sure enough, there was a crackling of branches as someone approached. He pressed his body to the damp ground, trying to blend into the peaty earth. There was a pause as the searchers listened for any movement. He held his breath. There was a crash and a shout.

"Hey Bobby, any sign of him?"

"Doesn't look as if he came this way!"

The crashing sound approached the silent boy. He flattened himself, burrowing into the rotting leaves, burying his hot sweaty face in the moist coolness of the soil. "

"Try over there, in those trees," shouted the first voice. John lifted his head very slightly and peered through the tangle of mossy roots and barbed brambles. He could see a pair of green Wellington boots, the toes pointing towards him. That was good -his seeker was Bob Procter, not Toby Watt, for Watt had black boots, and Bob was the one who would avoid any bits of wood where he might get hurt.

John was sure that if he could stay still long enough, he'd have a good chance of getting away. He closed his eyes and waited.

Fifteen miles from where John crouched in the undergrowth, Amy Meakin tightened the girth on her lively chestnut mare. Although it was still wet underfoot, the spring deluge of the past couple of weeks seemed to have passed, leaving clean washed, pale blue skies and scrubbed hedgerows.

"Easy lady," she murmured as the mare swung her rump sideways, tossing her mane with a loud snort. The animal was eager to set off. It had been impossible to go riding during the bad weather and the animal had been bored, but now the sun shone warmly and both horse and rider were raring to go.

"What time will you be back?"

Graham watched his wife as he checked the girth. He didn't share her delight in horses and always worried when she took the mare out over Dartmoor alone. Amy put her foot in the stirrup and swung herself up into the saddle.

"I'll be a couple of hours. I thought I'd go up past the quarry and give her a run on the flat up there."

With a wave of her hand, Amy kicked the mare forward. Graham watched them trotting down the lane, the mare's head held high, eager to get going.

* * *

John Crabb eased his cramped arm slightly to look at his watch. After crouching in the bushes for a good twenty minutes he decided it was safe to move. Carefully he eased himself up into a sitting position. He was cold, and his rumbling stomach informed him it was teatime. He grinned to himself, his freckled nose wrinkling, causing its coating of mud to flake off in patches. Just wait till he told them how close they'd been and still hadn't found him. He'd been unsure when boasting that none of them could find him when he hid, but he'd done it. He had proved it! Now he was stiff, hungry and the game had lost its charm. He stood up and stretched. There was a rustling sound on the bank above him and he guessed the others were over the rise. He waited for the shout of discovery, but nothing happened.

"Over here!" he yelled.

The rustling stopped suddenly but there was no answering yell. "Stop playing silly buggers," he shouted. "Game's over!" There was nothing, just silence. Or was there silence? John listened intently. He stepped out of the thicket and peered up the bank between the trees. There was a slight movement where the rustling was located, a slight shiver of newly opened leaves. Suddenly John felt very small and very alone. All around him was forestry land, the tall straight firs shutting out the sunlight, turning day into twilight.

"Stop mucking about," he yelled, but his voice sounded high-pitched and frightened. The woodland was no longer the familiar magic playground. It had suddenly become a dark and menacing place.

Branches cracked underfoot as whatever it was approached him. The breathing was louder, it was more like panting, and John knew with absolute certainty that it wasn't his friends up there on the slope.

Across the Devon moors, a few miles from where the boy stood rooted in fear, Amy Meakin leant over the mare's neck feeling the wind whipping back the coarse hair of its mane. She felt a wild sense of freedom as she crouched low in the saddle, the powerful muscles of her mount thrusting them both forward as the open moorland swept past. She turned the sweating animal back in a wide circle towards the disused quarry, reining in the mare as they approached the rocky path. The mare tossed her head and snorted, protesting at being slowed down from her headlong race, but obediently she eased her pace to a steady trot in response to her mistress's signals. They left the sunlight and entered the shady gloom of the woods. It was a peaceful place that Amy loved; the ground soft with its rotting carpet of last year's leaves, patches of creamy primroses resembling splashes of sunlight through the trees. The woods were a world of their own, a room that was forever changing the wallpaper. In January it had been a world of cotton wool and crystal, everything buried under a blanket of snow and ice. Now, in February, the melting snow was replaced by shivering snowdrops and pale primroses. Soon the carpet would be golden with daffodils, then blue with drooping bluebells, followed by summer green, foxglove pinks, and the autumn russets, reds and golds before finally the earth hues would give away to winter white and the paint brush would dip back into the palette for the yearly cycle to begin again.

Amy relaxed.

Without warning, came the scream.

The mare whinnied with fear, throwing back her head as she abruptly came to a halt, her ears laid back, her eyes rolling, showing white. Amy clung on, almost unseated as the animal reared up.

"Whoah there! Easy! Easy, girl!" The sweating animal danced backwards, snorting with terror. "Get on there. Walk on. Walk on, girl it's all right."

But it was not all right for the mare. The animal reared violently and sidestepped, refusing to obey the forward instruction. Amy clouted the mare with her crop, and dug her heels deeply into the heaving sides to show her anger, but the mare accepted the wrath in preference to moving towards whatever it was that terrified her. As they backed a little way down the path Amy at last regained control, but although the mare calmed down, nothing would induce her to move ahead. Amy patted the animal's sweaty neck to soothe it and looked around for the cause of fear. There was no cloth or plastic bag waving from a branch, no brightly covered object lying discarded by the path. Then Amy remembered the sound. Her immediate concern had been to stay in the saddle, and control the mare, and only now did she remember hearing the unearthly scream. She gazed uneasily around her while the mare stared ahead nervously, as if waiting for something that was hovering just out of sight.

"Kids!" she muttered angrily. "It must have been kids playing." She patted the mare's neck. "It's all right, they won't hurt you." If I could get my hands on the little brats, she thought. I'd give them screaming.

From the bushes on the slope above the path came the sound that Amy found impossible to describe afterwards. It was a cross between a screech and a wail, and was too much for the mare, who reared so violently that Amy had no chance. Unseated, she hurtled backwards off the mare as the animal twisted and with a shrill cry, kicking out her back hooves, thundered off along the path the way they had come. Amy seemed to fall in slow motion, seeing the ground rise towards her. Then she hit with a sickening crash, knocking the wind from her lungs. She lay stunned for a few seconds, the horrible wail echoed by her own scream ringing through the trees. As she lay still in a crumpled heap, fighting for breath, terrified that she had broken her back, there was a movement in the bushes above her, something horribly inhuman was coming towards her. She couldn't cry out, call for help, she could only struggle to draw air into bruised lungs, gasping like a stranded fish as whatever it was drew closer. She could hear the snapping of twigs as a large body pushed through the undergrowth. There was another sound even more unnerving than the shriek, the sound of heavy breathing, louder even than her own frantic gasps. Amy tried to crawl backwards, away from whatever it was, but her body wouldn't respond. As the bushes parted, Amy screamed and screamed…

Far away, John Crabb was also screaming as he crashed through the bushes, running for his life. Brambles clutched at his legs and tore his skin but he didn't notice them. He was only conscious of the sound of a heavy body bounding after him through the woods. The others heard him coming, and thought he was fooling around as they waited for him in the clearing where they usually played. Bob was suspended from an old tyre that hung from a broad-spreading oak in the centre of their camp, while the others were huddled together, having quiet puffs from a shared cigarette stolen from an unsuspecting parent. They all looked up as John tumbled into the clearing, his face bloody and scratched, the tears furrowing the mud on his cheeks.

"Run! For God's sake run!" he screamed.

They all leapt up in shock, Bob swinging himself down from the rope.

"What the hell…! exclaimed Toby.

"Run! Run!" cried John, but he could go no further, collapsing in a sobbing heap, his chest feeling as if it was on fire, his ribs seeming to smash into his lungs.

"What's happened?" asked Gary, dropping down beside John. "What is it?"

John couldn't answer. He choked and pointed back the slope behind him. They all followed his shaking finger.

"Oh, shit!" breathed Bob. The others said nothing. The only sounds were John's sobbing gasps and the heavy panting that came from the creature standing on the ridge above them, its body a black shadow against the light of the sky.

For a moment they stayed frozen, rooted to the spot with fear, then Bob yelled. "Run!"

And run they did, dragging an almost unconscious John with them. The beast made no attempt to follow, but the woods about it rang with a terrible scream that seemed to come from the jaws of hell.

* * *

Brian Henderson sat back and studied the soggy carton half filled with cold, scummy coffee from the office machine. Sometimes he wondered why he ever bothered to waste the money in the first place; he never drank the revolting stuff. It was force of habit really that sent him dutifully out into the corridor every couple of hours to feed the monster and watch it spew up the dark brown, lukewarm bile into the waiting dented paper cup. Sometimes he considered bringing a flask to work with real hot coffee, but somehow thinking about it was the nearest he ever got to committing the act itself. Thinking about such things epitomised the whole of Brian Henderson's life up to now. While he was thinking about them, the opportunities passed him by, and by the time he had decided that something was a good idea, it was already a very old idea, and someone else had usually had it and done something about it. Brian was just passed forty-years of age; he had made a brilliant start to his career as a cub reporter, but somewhere along the way he had lost the edge, the ambition, becoming a hack, without noticing the fact. He was still quite a good-looking man, his dark brown hair greying at the temples, his gut slightly bulging, but not yet hanging, over his trousers. He accepted that he was going to seed, but he wasn't yet ripe and hoped he was a long way from it.

He let his thoughts drift back to the task in hand. A clutter of yellowing newspaper clippings were scattered about his desk. Dating from the early eighties, the dramatic headlines were a memory of a media circus that had once made the Devon country lanes familiar to an international public.

For months readers had been held spellbound by the news that a ferocious big cat was roaming the West Country moors, striking silently and swiftly at night, leaving a trail of bloody sheep carcasses in its wake.

Brian studied the reports of what became known as the Exmoor Beast Hunt. Farmers had been demanding protection for their grazing flocks until the situation became so fraught that the local police finally requested help from the Royal Marine Commandos. It was the involvement of the Special Forces that had caught the imagination of the world's media. Questions were asked in both Houses of Parliament, television crews filled the lanes and the *Exeter Times* enjoyed its moment of glory. Yet despite the intervention of the government and the involvement of the armed forces, the beast, or beasts, had remained at large. After the marines and the media had gone home, and the locals returned to their peaceful life, farmers still lost stock and occasionally a witness reported seeing a big cat on the moors, but the Exmoor Beast became part of moorland folklore.

It was one of these new big cat sightings that had arrived on Brian's desk during the week. As there wasn't much else to follow up, perhaps he could dig up some background and run a new beast story around the report.

"Seeing Angie and the kids this weekend?"

Tom Bates, the paper's photographer, put his head around the door and grinned cheerfully. Angie was Brian's former wife and he was ever hopeful that the two would get back together again.

"Nope." Brian stretched and yawned. "She's taking the kids up to stay with her mother for a week." His relationship with Angie had seemed the one real successful thing in his life until it started going wrong as the result of too many nights propping up the bars with colleagues, and too few nights spent home with his family. He knew he'd been at fault, and knew Angie's accusations were all true. He had made umpteen vows to change his ways, and to keep office hours, but somehow he never seemed able to refuse that quick pint after work, and could never say no to his mates. In the end, it was Angie who said no.

No to their marriage.

The thing that shocked Brian was that it didn't change his way of life at all. True, he no longer went home to cooked meals, but then he seldom had anyway. Although he now had to do his own laundry, tidying his own bachelor pad when he ran out of floor space, and washing up when he ran out of clean cups. He ate mainly in pubs and cafés and bought drip-dry, non-iron shirts and there was no comment if his sheets did look rather grey, or his collars a little grubby. It boiled down to the fact that Brian Henderson was a slob, and quite happy as one.

Although he had failed as a husband, he wanted to succeed as a father. They were his Achilles heel, his children; Shane aged ten and Karen seven. To them it mattered how he behaved, and because it mattered to them, it mattered to him. He could accept failure in everything except his kids' eyes, because he loved them.

Tom pushed aside the mass of crumpled papers to sit on the edge the desk. "What's new?"

Brian shrugged. "Not a lot. War is about to breakout and the pope admits smoking pot." He stretched his arms behind his head and yawned, the image of rushed, hard-hitting, embittered journalists being far removed from the reality of working for a small provincial newspaper. Tom picked up a report from the floor.

"What's this?"

Brian took it from him, glanced at it and then screwed up the copy to aim the ball at the newspaper basket. "That's yesterday's headliner. Seems like the beast of the moors is rearing its ghostly little head again. Some old biddy came a cropper off her horse over Manaton way and claims she was a victim of our furry friend."

"Bad?"

"She'd probably have fared worse coming off a bike. Seems she got a couple of busted ribs and a broken leg. Mind you, she was lucky the husband was there when the horse came home without her and he sounded the alarm. If she'd have been out overnight, she might have made the obituary column. The hospital says she's comfortable, though how anyone can be described as comfortable in those circumstances beats me. They think she might have concussion though, raving on about lions."

"Thought it was supposed to be a puma?"

Brian grinned. "Lion or puma? What's the difference? They are all just big pussycats. Makes a change from pink elephants I suppose." He stood up and took his coat off the back of his chair. "Fancy a lunchtime pint?"

Together they walked out of the door, ignoring the frantic ringing of the telephone behind them.

Jim Bowers put down the 'phone with a sigh. He guessed where Brian was. Damn! He wanted to send Brian out, but there was no real urgency, he supposed. He only needed a few lines on a couple of kids claiming to have been attacked by a black panther near Widdicombe. Probably a load of balls, just a bit of fertile imagination and a big dog at best. Still a new beast story could liven up the paper a bit. He'd get Brian after lunch. He went back to his job as editor of the *Exeter Times*, reading the copy for the following day's edition. It was a far from enthralling read.

Later that afternoon, Brian was sitting rather disinterestedly, listening to young John Crabb's graphic description of the beast they had seen in the forest two days before.

"About how big was it?"

"Bigger than a dog," John assured him excitedly, the fear of the moment forgotten. He was thoroughly enjoying all the attention he was getting.

Brian smiled. "Dogs," he pointed out rather fairly, "come in a variety of sizes."

"A big dog," John assured him." Bigger than any dog around here."

"A collie? An Alsatian or even a great dane?"

John thought seriously for a moment, then shook his head. "It wasn't as big as a great dane, 'cause it was not so tall. More like an Alsatian but a bit longer, I think, with a real heavy body."

Brian jotted down notes on his pad. He still used old-fashioned methods, preferring to rely on his own shorthand rather than the modern micro recorders. "But you say it wasn't a dog?"

"It wasn't like no dog I've ever seen," said John firmly. "It was a huge cat, like a puma or a panther. It had a flat cat-like face and it yowled like a cat. It didn't bark or anything like that."

"It was a cat, mister," Toby Watt confirmed, with approving nods from other boys. "A bloody great cat, and it scared the hell out of me." Toby was the eldest of the boys, a sensible twelve. Brian looked at him with interest.

"There's absolutely no doubt in your mind that it wasn't a dog?"

Toby shook his head. "We all got a fairly good look at it," he answered frankly. "Course, we didn't see as much of it as Johnny here, but I know what a dog looks like, and I know what a cat looks like, and that there animal was a cat."

"What sort of cat?"

Toby frowned in concentration. "It's sort of hard to say, but it were dark with prickled ears. Really powerful looking."

Brian produced a number of photographs he had collected from the office, a lioness, a puma, a leopard, and a lynx among them. He fanned them out across the farmhouse table. "Anything like any of these?"

The boys sifted through the photographs carefully, then without a word, they selected one which they laid before him.

"It's not exact," explained Toby, "but that's the nearest."

"The one we saw were black though, and I think its legs were a bit shorter," added John with a slight shiver. "But it had a face just like that."

Brian looked at the photograph which showed a North American puma standing on a boulder, snarling its defiance at the camera.

"You're all sure that's what you saw and not a dog?" he asked. The boys nodded in unison. "Yeah, that's the nearest to the cat what chased us."

Brian picked up the pictures. He was sceptical of the boys' story. Despite the years of tales of big cats roaming the moors, there had never been any actual proof. No bodies had ever been found, and no identifiable photographs taken. Just rumours and stories. There was nothing new in the boys' account, and their description was no doubt coloured by previous reports. All the same, as he looked down at the photograph, he wondered. Despite the numerous official and unofficial hunts failing to produce any hard evidence, the eager young faces around him made him feel uneasy.

CHAPTER 2

H e was still wondering later while seated in the *Fox and Hounds*, the local watering hole for the staff of the *Exeter Times* and a first home to Brian Henderson. Beside him, Jim Bowers stared intently at his own pint of amber frothy bitter.

"Oh come on, Brian. They're only kids. Too much imagination and too long school holidays. They're having you on."

Brian stared at his pasty and shrugged. "Could be," he agreed, "but I don't know, I've got a gut feeling they're not. I can't put my finger on it, but I think they're telling the truth."

"As they see it."

"Maybe. But they did pick out the puma, not as dramatic as a lion or a leopard. And people do keep pumas as pets. Isn't it possible that someone let one loose up the forest when it became a liability or cost too much to feed?"

"That has always been the story, of course. That someone dumped a big cat because of the 1976 Dangerous Wild Animals Act," Tom Bates spoke seriously. He had been with the *Exeter Times* even longer than Brian, and he was fast heading for his gold watch. He was still the best news photographer around, despite failing health and limited opportunity.

"Suppose someone had dumped an unwanted puma," muttered Brian, "there's plenty of deer and sheep to keep it going, and let's face it, hardly anyone ever goes up there, not even the foresters - just kids playing and the odd hunter or poacher. Not exactly overcrowding, is it?"

Jim sipped his pint appreciably. "Sorry I still don't buy it. If it's been around since 1976, it would have died of old age long ago."

"But there have been reports of attacks on stock for years," Brian reasoned.

"Dogs." Jim wasn't going to be persuaded easily. Tom chewed the end of his battered pipe.

"Farmers have told me they've found sheep carcasses stripped clean as a whistle. Some were so pissed off they've gone out nights on armed patrols."

"The only thing they'd shoot is each other," snorted Jim.

"Ah come on, Jim. There's nothing much happening at the moment," Brian pleaded. "It's worth a few days to investigate, surely? Look at the mileage got out of the previous beast hunts. And they never did catch the blighters."

"If they ever existed anywhere, other than in some reporter's fertile little cesspit brain," Jim sighed. "Still we might get a bit of copy from it, if you can find a new angle."

"Then I can spend a few days digging around?" asked Brian eagerly, surprised by how enthusiastic he was feeling. He was a news hound again with the scent in his nostrils.

"A few hours," said Jim firmly. Instead of paying Brian to sit on his backside with his feet on the desk, he might as well have him on a wild goose chase and at least doing something active for his wages. The only financial loss to the paper would be a cut in the profits from the coffee machine.

"Fair enough, a few hours." To Brian's flexible mind, a few hours could range from three to three-hundred-and-thirty-three, so he wasn't going to argue the point.

Tom looked up. "It's my shout, I think," he said, surveying the usual litter of empty glasses on their table. The others didn't argue. "Might do well to start with your fallen equestrian," he muttered.

"His what?" echoed Jim.

"Brian's heard about some old biddy who reckoned a lion made her fall off her horse."

Jim looked sharply at Brian. "I don't remember reading the copy."

"That's because it wasn't anything like that old shit-stirrer's making out. Just some woman raving about lions after a riding accident. Hospital put it down to concussion."

Jim grunted. "Sure it isn't catching?" he asked sarcastically, but Brian wasn't biting.

The following morning found Brian standing in the sister's office at the orthopaedic ward of Exeter General Hospital. The sister was young, blond and pretty, far removed from the traditional sister image of huge bosom and starched face.

"I'm not sure that Doctor will allow you to see Mrs Meakin, even if the patient is willing to talk to you. She has been very poorly and we don't want her upset." The sister smiled.

"I won't say anything to disturb Mrs Meakin. In normal circumstances, I wouldn't bother her at all." He paused, "It's just something I want to check on." He matched smile for smile while he wondered what she was doing that night. Then he spotted the gold band on her finger.

"And that is?"

Brian pushed aside the vision of the sister with her blonde hair falling loose, her soft breasts swinging free from the restraint of their firm starchy uplift. He tore his eyes from the outline of her nipples and tried to concentrate on the matter in hand.

"It's just something she is reported to have said when she came round, something about seeing big cats."

Sister shrugged. "Well, she was rambling. She has had a nasty fall."

"But did she talk about seeing big cats?"

Sister smiled again. "People talk about all sorts of things when they are regaining consciousness."

"But did Mrs Meakin talk about cats?" Brian persisted.

Sister looked pointedly at her watch. "I believe she did say something of the sort. Now I do have a very heavy workload. We've three going to theatre this afternoon." She opened the door of her office and gestured to a seat by the lift. "If you wouldn't mind taking a seat outside until I can get a doctor to speak to you?"

"Thank you. I'm sorry to have taken up your time, sister, but it might be important." Brian turned to leave the office.

"What, Mrs Meakin's delusions?"

He paused. "If they are delusions? You must know that there have been many reports of cats on the moors over the years, and now a group of children say they were attacked by a big cat on the same day that Mrs Meakins had her accident. Probably just coincidence, but…?"

The sister laughed. "You lot still beast hunting, are you? I thought that had been disproved years ago. Well, you'd better talk to Doctor about it." She grinned. "Wouldn't like to think we might be getting customers with a few chunks missing. While you are waiting, I'll go and ask the patient if she'll agree to see you, providing Doctor lets her."

Fifteen minutes later, Brian was back in sister's office, seated opposite a fresh-faced, young looking houseman whose badge proclaimed him to be Dr Tateman. The doctor scanned the file in front of him and then looked up.

"Mrs Meakin was in a poor condition when she was first brought in. She had been lying for some hours before she was discovered. Unfortunately, it seems she had managed to crawl into the bushes before passing out so she was hidden from view to anyone walking along the path. It was only when the police tracker dogs were called in that she was found, by which time she was suffering from severe shock and exposure."

"And when she came round she spoke of seeing big cats?"

Dr Tateman nodded. "Of course, we put it down to concussion, but it might be useful to have a little chat with the patient to see if she can remember any more." He picked up the file and stood up. "If you'd like to come with me?" He led the way out of the office. "I would like to emphasise that if Mrs Meakin shows any sign of distress then the interview must be terminated at once." Brian nodded. "Please keep your questions brief."

Amy Meakin was in a side ward; a bright airy room, her locker overflowing with flowers and get well cards. She was lying almost flat, her lower body encased in plaster and partly suspended from the metal framework bolted to the bed. Seeing her in traction reminded Brian of a puppet dangling from strings.

She looked up and smiled. "Hallo, Doctor."

"Good morning, Mrs Meakin," he said brightly, while checking the charts at the foot of the bed." And how are you feeling today?"

"A bit sore but mainly bored," she said with a rueful grin.

"Ah, well, perhaps we can do something about that. I've brought someone who wants to have a chat with you about the accident. Do you feel up to talking?"

"Yes, sister told me." Amy looked curiously at Brian.

"This is Mr Henderson." The doctor waved him to a bedside chair.

Brian said, "Hi.... Morning." He felt uncomfortable. It was like being in a stranger's bedroom, and he always hated hospitals. The smell alone made him feel sick. There was an aura of human misery and despair about them. Statistics might show that most operations were fairly minor and most patients went home cured, but there was always the knowledge that some didn't, and within the antiseptic and imposing walls, some lives were condemned and others ended.

"Mr Henderson is a reporter for the *Exeter Times* and he is interested in some of what you told us when you first came around after your accident."

Amy grinned cheerfully. "Oh dear, Mr Henderson. I do hope I wasn't terribly indiscreet. Am I going to end up in your gossip column and then be sued for libel?"

Brian instinctively liked Amy, who seemed a sensible young woman, a far cry from his picture of an old biddy. "No, nothing so exciting." He sat down and took out his dog-eared notebook.

"Can you tell Mr Henderson anything you can remember about the accident?" asked the doctor. Amy looked towards Dr Tateman, and was reassured by his encouraging smile.

"It's all a bit of a muddle really, a hazy muddle at that. As you know, when I came round, I believe I was raving and gave everyone a bit of a hard time. I kept seeing lions and wanted to get out of bed." She laughed rather self-consciously.

"According to Mrs Meakin, we were all going to be devoured in our beds." Dr Tateman patted her hand. "That's why we put her in here. She had a rather disrupting influence on the rest of the patients."

Amy blushed. "Oh dear, was I as bad as that?"

The doctor grinned. "You were a little incoherent," he said. "If it's going to make you feel any better, that's why Mr Henderson is here. He wants to ask you about the lions you kept seeing. At least, what you can remember about them."

Amy looked surprised. "But you say I was rambling. I can't really remember very much."

"It's not what happened after you reached the hospital that interests me," Brian said gently. "I want to know about the lions you saw?"

Amy shrugged and then winced as the movement hurt. "Well, it's difficult to know what was real and what wasn't. I seem to remember seeing one, and hearing it scream. That's why my horse bolted, because something screamed."

"Something?" asked Brian quietly.

Amy frowned. "Yes. Everything was normal. The ride was just as usual except that the mare was a little frisky, not having been out for a few days because of the weather. We'd just got to the wood when she suddenly reared up in fright and started dancing all over the place."

"And that is when you came off?" prompted Brian. Amy shook her head.

"No. I regained control, but I couldn't get her to go ahead. I couldn't see anything wrong but she was snorting and prancing about as though terrified. It was then I heard it." She put her hand up to her ears as though the echoes remained to haunt her.

"What?"

She shook her head. "That's just it, I don't know. It was a terrible scream, like nothing I've ever heard before. It made your hair stand on end, it really did. That's when I came off. I wasn't expecting it and had loosened my grip. Silly, really. It was all so quick. The mare just went up in the air as though she was on springs, and then she was away. I could hear the screaming even as I fell, then I must have hit the ground because everything is in bits and pieces. I must have been stunned but when I came to, there was something thrashing about in the bushes near me, something that was breathing heavily. It was horrible. I wanted to get away but I couldn't move, and I couldn't scream, and it was getting closer. It was like a terrible nightmare and I was trapped in the middle of it."

There was distress in her voice and fear in her eyes as she paused. Brian looked at Dr Tateman, who patted her hand reassuringly.

"Would you rather not talk about it anymore?" he asked soothingly.

She shook her head. "No, no, it's all right, really it is. Talking about it might help put the whole thing into perspective, if you know what I mean."

"A little longer then," agreed the doctor. He signalled across to Brian to speed things up.

"Did you see what was coming towards you?" Brian asked quietly. Amy nodded.

"I think so." She paused, then added, with a slight tremor in her voice. "Everyone seems to think I got whacked on the head and imagined the lot. But as God is my judge, I swear that a bloody great lion walked out of the bushes and came up to sniff me."

"You say it was a lion?"

Amy was silent for a few moments as she gazed thoughtfully out of the window, then she turned to Brian. "I don't know a lot about big cats. It was brown, but it didn't have a mane, so it was like a lioness. I can't remember any more until I came round here after my operation. I suppose I must have passed out cold."

Brian stared at his pad. "Do you think you imagined the animal or do you think you really saw it?"

Amy looked at Dr Tateman. "I expect I'm asking to be locked away for saying this, but no, I don't think I imagined it. I'm damn sure I really did see the creature." She sighed. "I mean I've heard about the beast stories but I never believed in them, not until now."

Brian looked across at the doctor. "I'd like her to look at a few pictures, if that's okay. Then I'm through." Dr Tateman nodded and Brian took some photographs from his pocket and fanned them out across the bed where Amy could see them. They were the same photographs he had shown to the boys. "Did you see anything like any of these?" he asked.

Amy studied each photograph closely; then she gave a slight shudder. "That's it!" she exclaimed firmly and passed the picture of the puma to him, the same photograph that the boys had chosen.

"And you say it was brown?"

Amy was still staring with horrified fascination at the puma as Brian began to collect up the photographs. He paused before adding the one of the puma and then thrust them all, with his note pad, back into his pocket.

"Thank you, Mrs Meakin. You've been a great help." He paused and smiled. "And if it's any help to you, I don't think you imagined the beast at all, I think you really saw it. Some other witnesses have reported seeing a puma out in the woods on the same day that you had your accident. It was a few miles away, but as the crow flies," he grinned, "or as the cat runs, I suppose it wasn't so far."

Amy looked at him. "You mean you think I did actually see it?" she asked. He nodded. She leant back and closed her eyes. "Thank God," she whispered to herself. "I really thought I must be going mad." For the first time since the accident, she wasn't afraid to fall asleep.

Later that day, Brian leant back from the keyboard and stretched his aching shoulders. To his amazement, he realised he hadn't the usual surrounding debris of squashed half-filled coffee cups, but then, for a change, he hadn't been bored by his own article. He pulled the sheet from the printer and scanned over it thoughtfully.

"The beast is back."

The headline certainly made more interesting reading than the normal copy, though he doubted if Jim would give it the column space it deserved. He was right.

"I can't print this as fact. Sightings are old hat. I told you to find a new angle!"

Brian tried to keep the irritation out of his voice. "I don't write it as fact, I just look at the possibility of feral big cats. After all, you know how many rumours there have been of escaped exotic animals. Wild boars, and even bears, have been reported from time to time. And we know that porcupines are living and breeding on the outskirts of Okehampton. Why not, a solitary puma?"

"But you've not come up with anything new. I'm sorry, Brian, I know you've got a bee in your bonnet about this, but it's a no go. Not without more to go on than a couple of kids and a woman who's had a bad knock on the head."

Brian sighed. "Fair enough."

* * *

Pruned down, the article was hardly noticeable when it appeared later that week:

> On Thursday, four young boys, aged eleven and twelve, playing in the woods near High Torre, reported seeing an animal they later identified as a puma. They told the police the animal approached them but did not give chase when they ran away.
>
> It is believed the same animal might have been responsible for a riding accident on the same afternoon.
>
> Mrs Amy Meakin, Broadstone Farm, Torwell, was thrown from her horse near Whitstone Quarry suffering serious injury. Mrs Meakin told the *Exeter Times* that her horse had been startled by a loud scream. She saw a puma-like animal in the undergrowth after her horse bolted.
>
> The horse returned to the farm where the alarm was raised. Mrs Meakin was found by a search party and is expected to remain in hospital for a few weeks where her condition is said to be comfortable.
>
> A police spokesman stated that it was probably a rogue dog responsible for both incidents. They also believe the animal is responsible for a spate of sheep worrying in the area.

Farmer Tim Parker, however, wasn't thinking of dogs as he stood looking down at all that remained of one of his prize Suffolk ewes.

"Darn me," he muttered as he kicked at the carcass with his wellington boot. "Darn me if it hasn't been ate. The whole bloody lot!"

Later that night, in the public bar of the *Rose and Crown*, he gazed morosely into his pint. "I'll tell you, Jack, I ain't seen nothing like it in all my born days. Ate, it was, clean as a whistle."

"Pesky buggering foxes," muttered Jack as he set down the next round. "Shoot the bloody lot of the bastards, that's what."

"Clean as a whistle," sighed Tim. "Nothing but bones and bloody skin! Yet I'll swear blind it was alive yesterday morning. I saw the ewe myself." He frowned. "Some bugger ate the lot!"

Jack nodded. "Reminds me of the trouble they had on Exmoor a few years back. Stock killed and ate nightly. Never did get the bastard."

"Well, I bloody hope the sod is not using me as the local snack bar," Tim said in a loud voice while he stared gloomily into his beer. No one took any notice. After all, farmers were always complaining about something.

CHAPTER 3

Brian paused, puffing and blowing from the unaccustomed exercise and studied his map. In print it had looked a brisk and easy walk, but the reality had proved a long hard slog for muscles more used to operating accelerator, brake and clutch pedals, than striding across the Devon countryside. He wiped the sweat off his face and rubbed his aching neck, although why his neck should ache when his legs had been doing all the work was beyond his comprehension. He was shocked to realise he was in such poor physical condition, and made a sincere mental note to start considering a fitness programme when he had time.

He stared ahead over the dried remains of last year's bracken, seeing the jumble of boulders ahead with relief, for the scattering of stone revealed the proximity of the quarry, the landmark for which he was searching. With a deep breath, he slowly descended the slippery path, the camera swinging around his neck like a lead weight. By the time he reached the quarry, the camera had definitely increased in weight and his aches had doubled. He refused to consider that he had to walk all the way back to reach his car; it was a fact of life that simply did not bear thinking about, like approaching death or infinity. He paused to regain his breath and looked around him. The walls towered above him, sheer slippery blocks of stone, while the floor was heaped in scree and flaking dark grey slate embedded in sticky brick red clay and grit.

It was many years since the quarry had been worked, but the evidence of man's hand was clear to see, the walls revealing blast marks and some hewn and hacked rocky slate lying tumbled, waiting to be removed by craftsmen who would never return. Other slabs were only partly shaped, still attached to the mother rock's umbilical cord like giant steps leading to the sky. The only signs of life were a couple of moorland sheep that searched hopefully for spring grass among the rubble, and a huge buzzard that hovered lazily overhead, its powerful wings stretched to catch the currents of wind, its bright eyes watching the sweating man as he watched it. In such isolated surroundings, it was easy to believe in the existence of a big cat living wild. With a slight shiver Brian visualised the sleek powerful beast crouched high on the rocky ledges, its lips curled in a snarl to reveal curved white fangs, its eyes clear and intense, studying him. He had read up on pumas and knew they weren't supposed to be dangerous to man, a fact that had made them popular pets in the sixties, but out on the moors, alone and unarmed he felt tiny and puny, the security of written facts lost to the reality of the situation. Had the writers ever put their theories to the test, he wondered? He doubted it, and doubt did nothing for his sense of security.

Brian moved on quickly, glad to get past the sinister, barren, quarry. Although the woods could hide a waiting predator just as successfully as the tumbled stone, there was something less threatening about the budding trees and primrose scattered glades. He moved slowly along the muddy path, his feet sinking into the squelchy carpet of rotting leaves, and he wondered where Amy Meakin had actually had her accident. A few muddy tracks could be seen in the sticky clay - dogs, horses and ribbed boots - but he was surprised to find wheel marks, until he remembered the Landrover. Of course, he was seeing the evidence of the rescue party. He finally reached the area in which it was obvious Amy had been found. Here he paused and stared around at the smashed and flattened bushes.

The ground was churned up and the confused tyre marks showed where the driver had reversed in a multiple point turn on the restricted narrow pathway. It was a particularly dense piece of woodland, the trees growing close together, blotting out the light, and a tangle of ground ivy and briars covered the earth as it banked upwards on either side into steep slopes. He picked up a broken branch and attempted to push his way into the dense undergrowth, the brambles gripping at his trouser legs as he hauled himself upwards, looking for any sign of a trail or animal tracks. The deep peaty carpet of last season's leaves finally defeated him.

Feeling bruised and battered, he reached the crest of the ridge from where he could look down on to the path. It had been from this ridge that Amy Meakin claimed the animal had come. She remembered hearing it moving towards her on the left. Brian studied the ground carefully. There was a track along the highest point, not one that had been trampled by countless human feet, but a narrow path through the undergrowth made by the constant passage of animals, perhaps deer or sheep. He moved slowly along it, studying the ground intently, remembering enough from his Boy Scout days to recognise fox and badger prints, although he couldn't be certain whether the numerous small v-shaped marks were deer slots or wandering sheep. It was then that he spotted the dog prints.

Or were they?

He crouched down and examined them closely. They were large, measuring a good four inches across, showing a broad crescent-shaped heel pad with four toe pads spaced evenly around the heel, the deep impressions of the claws clearly visible. Whatever had walked along the path had been large and very heavy, judging by the depth of the prints and spacing between them, almost great dane size. Yet there was no evidence of a human walker exercising his pet. Brian straightened up. From the height of the ridge he had a clear view for miles of the surrounding countryside, confirming his suspicion that there was no human habitation for some distance. It seemed doubtful that a dog the size of a great dane would be wandering alone so far from home. He bent down again and examined the prints closely. They were the right size but the wrong shape for a large dog. He moved back along the path a little to check out some fox tracks. These were the right for a dog-like animal, the four toes set a distance ahead of the heel pad, not neatly arranged around it. Even to Brian, the big prints looked unlike those of a dog. They reminded him of outsize versions of the household tabby.

Brian felt a chill as he photographed the clearest prints, all the while listening for any movement in the bushes around him, then fearfully and quickly he slithered back down the bank to the main path and headed out of the wooded area. He made his way back passed the quarry, ignoring the pain in his chest and the ache in his legs and only breathed freely when he finally reached the safety and security of his car. He felt a little foolish about his panic, but whatever had walked across the ridge, he hadn't fancied making its close acquaintance. As he drove home wearily, he began to think clearly, and at once he felt a thrill as the adrenaline started to flow. He had always dismissed beast stories as a combination of myth and fiction, but whatever had walked along the woodland path had been no myth. It had been flesh and blood.

And big.

* * *

Mrs Agnes Briant peered nervously out of her window; it was still dark and only the flat open area of the large lawn showed light as the moon hung like a huge pale globe in the purple blackness of the sky. She looked at her clock - it was just five-thirty, and old Mrs Briant was very tired, but she couldn't sleep. She heaved herself painfully out of the chair and hobbled stiffly to the kitchen where the kettle hummed softly as steam began to spiral upwards. A nice cup of tea, that's what she needed. With shaking hands she spooned loose tea leaves from the old fashioned caddy; she didn't approve of the modern dust-filled teabags. Whatever the adverts said, it was not the same thing - more like drinking washing-up water instead of a good strong cuppa. Her arthritic-bent fingers curled round the kettle handle, wobbling slightly as she filled the pot. She sniffed appreciatively at the aromatic steam that rose around her as she carried the pot into the lounge and settled again into her chair, the cup rattling slightly against the saucer as she poured. She glanced at the clock, it was nearly six, almost time. She stared out of the window thoughtfully as she sipped her tea.

Outside, the shrubbery rustled as something moved through the rhododendrons, something that pushed gently past the black leafy shadows. Agnes Briant didn't hear the rustle of branches, but she sensed it was coming; it was time, the sky was lighter and even her tired old eyes could make out the garden shapes clearly in the dawn illumination. She put down her cup quietly and stared intently towards the blackness of the bushes at the end of her lawn. She couldn't see the movement, she only saw the light from the eyes, but that was the way it always was, the glow of the eyes reflecting the light from the window like twin burning coals. Silently the animal moved out of the shadows, its long sleek body rippling along the ground in a snake-like motion as it padded forward, its large velvety feet making no sound as they touched the dew-wet grass until it reached the tiny ornamental fishpond. There it crouched, its shoulder blades sharply outlined against the pink tinged sky as its head and neck sunk down, its tongue lapping noisily at the silver water, droplets sparkling like diamonds. Having drunk its fill, the beast lifted its head and stared directly at the house. Mrs Briant was sure it was staring at her before it turned and, within a blink of an eye, was gone.

As the garden grew lighter and vision clearer, the old lady pushed aside her cup, satisfied. Whatever they said, whatever they all thought, she wasn't mad. Every morning at about the same time, the black beast visited her, a sleek black panther with glowing eyes. Once, a year ago, or perhaps it had been two? Time sometimes became muddled when she tried to remember events - she had actually seen the beast in daylight. She had been out weeding the garden one sunlit afternoon when she heard a strange cry, almost a scream, coming from the woodland. Curious, she'd put down her gardening fork and struggled to her feet to walk stiffly over the grass in the direction of the sound. As she reached the sprawling copper beech hedge, she heard the cry again, a wild unearthly scream like nothing she had ever heard before. Frightened, she had peered through the bronze leaves into the woodland that spread right up to her land, surrounding her garden. Ahead of her was a small clearing where years before the wind had felled three great trees, leaving a grass-filled hollow.

Agnes Briant had pushed the branches aside to gain a better view. Then she had frozen in horror, too terrified to move or make a sound. The rotting trunk of one of the trees still lay where it had fallen, although all its smaller branches had long ago found their way into the old lady's stove, and seated on the stripped tree was a huge black cat. The animal had its back to her, its head was lifted to the sky, its ears laid back and from its snarling mouth came the unearthly screech she had heard. There had been no doubt in her mind that the animal was a black panther, it was definitely a cat the size of an Alsation dog, with a long thick tail that twitched and lashed from side to side, hitting the wood with hollow thuds. Its glossy sleek coat was short haired and blue-black in colour in the bright sunlight, and the muscles rippled beneath the skin.

Gently Agnes Briant had replaced the twigs and quietly edged her way back across the lawn to the safety of the house, all thoughts of gardening forgotten for the day. Once indoors, she had telephoned the police. She talked to a polite sergeant who promised to send an officer round straight away. What she took to be immediately had stretched to become four hours, and by the time the policeman arrived, of course the cat was nowhere to be seen. However, he had taken a walk through the woods before assuring the frightened old lady that whatever she had seen was long gone.

"Now don't you worry, ma," he reassured her. "You just give us a ring if you see it again, but I expect it's moved on."

Agnes Briant wasn't at all sure it had gone, especially after hearing that terrible cry again a few weeks later during the night. When she considered it was a reasonable time, she did as she'd been told and once more 'phoned the police. Again they'd come, and again found nothing. Since then she had dutifully 'phoned the police whenever she saw the creature, and once she realised it made an almost nightly trip across her garden to drink from her fishpond, so her calls to the police became almost a daily event.

A creature of habit, like the beast she was so concerned about, that morning, she made her usual call.

At nine o'clock in the morning, the telephone rang in the small rural police station. P.C. John

Marker sighed and glanced at the circular wooden framed wall clock.

"Dead on time," he groaned, "regular as Big Ben is old ma Briant."

"I'll take it this morning," his colleague P.C. George Wells grinned. It had been Wells who had called on Mrs Briant all that time ago and, having made the drastic mistake of inviting her to call them, he felt a personal responsibility for the whole situation. He lifted the receiver and listened sympathetically for a few moments.

"Right, Mrs Briant, I've logged the sighting and as soon as I'm free I'll have a look round to make sure it's gone, I won't disturb you though, so don't worry." He paused. "Don't you fret, now, I'll be careful." He paused again and then added with a smile, "No I don't think I'll be armed, but don't you worry, we'll get him one of these days." He put the 'phone down and sighed. "Poor old duck," he said. "Must be lonely, being so isolated, living out there in that big house. They ought to put her in a home. She'd be better off, she would."

Agnes Briant had no thoughts of being better off in a home as, shaking a little, she made herself some toast for her breakfast. She loved her big house on the moors. Always had. It wasn't just a case of bricks and mortar; every room still echoed with memories, the sounds of a past family life. Time had dimmed many things for her, but not the distant years, which seemed more real to her than the present. When she walked through the shabby rooms of the house, her husband was still alive, her surviving children weren't scattered across the world. Sometimes, in her clearer moments, she understood and accepted the truth, but to live in memories was so much more pleasant than facing reality, and as long as she could live within her own home, she could also live in happier times.

* * *

Tim Purbect sat absentmindedly tapping a pencil on the desktop. If his workload was anything to go by in a country area, he certainly didn't envy his colleagues up in the big cities. He frowned as he looked at the file in front of him. Mrs Agnes Briant, a widow aged eighty-two, confused and beginning to make a nuisance of herself, constantly 'phoning the police and the council about imaginary panthers wandering all over the place. He sighed. He remembered the old lady very clearly; a nice old dear pottering about a big rambling house stuffed full of heavy dusty furniture and a clutter of memorabilia, very bright mentally though badly crippled with arthritis. It was sad that the mind of such a pleasant and well-educated woman should begin to go, but obviously it had for her to start seeing things. There was a solution of course, though Tim Purbect regretted being the person to take action leading to it. The old lady would be better off in a home. Trouble was, beds were not easy to find. He looked again at the file and the report from the police of the calls she had been making for months. It wouldn't be easy, but it had to be done. He lifted the 'phone and pressed the buttons with his chewed pencil.

* * *

That night Brian was propping up the bar in the *Fox and Hounds*, flanked by his colleagues from the *Exeter Times*.

"Oh come on, mate, you can't be serious."

"I'm telling you there were prints up there the size of my hand," Brian waved a hand in Jim's face to illustrate his point.

"A big dog?" suggested Tom, anxious to keep the peace.

"Of course it bloody was!" exclaimed Jim. "After all, we called in dogs for the search. From what I can gather, the poor woman would still have been there if it hadn't been for the dogs."

"But not up on the ridge," argued Brian. "They wouldn't have sent the dogs up on the ridge. It was too far away from the path where the search was carried out and the search dogs' prints were nothing like the damn great things I'm talking about. I tell you, man; they were a good four or five inches across. I'd like to meet the dog that could make those!"

Jim wasn't convinced. "Could have been a great dane. Or a St Bernard. Especially on soft ground."

Brian gazed at his empty glass. "It's pretty unlikely up there. Let's face it, people don't let the big pedigree dogs roam about like they do the mutts, and I'm telling you, it's wild up there, like a bloody jungle. In some of that woodland you could hide a herd of elephants."

Jim leant across the bar and waved the barman over, "Hey Steve, fill them up and shove it on my slate, will you?" It was a point of honour for Jim never actually to pay at the time of drinking. With his status as editor, he felt it impressed guests, made him appear like a hard-bitten pressman, worldly wise. Then nightly, at the end of a drinking session, if he were sober enough, he would settle up. If not, the till would have to wait patiently until the following lunchtime to be fed.

"Look, suppose you are right. Supposing the beast is real, that there is a big cat living up on the moors? So what? It's not actually killed anyone, has it? Just spooked a horse and put the fear of God into a couple of kids? So what's the big deal?" asked Tom quietly.

"Not one, but two. There are at least two beasts," said Brian calmly.

"Oh, come on now, be serious!" exploded Tom. "One I can accept. After all, the police have always considered the possibility. But only one."

"At least," repeated Brian calmly. "If a pair have been around since '76, and mated, we could easily have a dozen roaming around the moors, and if they breed - well, in twenty years or so we could be running bloody safari holidays around here."

The two other men looked at him in shocked silence.

"You are joking," said Jim coldly.

Brian shook his head. "I wish I was," he said.

"You know, there could be something in what he is saying."

All three looked at Steve Hockley, the barman.

"Don't you start," warned Jim, considering the joke had gone far enough. "Christ! If anyone overheard this conversation and passed it on to the uneducated masses, we'd have a bloody panic on our hands!"

"Maybe we should," said Steve seriously, dropping his voice to almost a whisper. "But I'm telling you, I've heard some damn strange things in this bar, not the least of which is people claiming to have seen all manner of weird animals out on the moors."

"What sort of animals?" asked Brian quickly.

Steve glanced around to check that no one else was listening. "I'm not saying that I believe in the tales, mind, but there are them that do and they aren't all cranks or idiots."

"But what have they seen?" asked Brian impatiently.

"Some as claim to have seen big cats up there - really big cats, the size of lions - for years."

"Do you think they are telling the truth?"

"Let's put it this way," Steve Hockley said earnestly. "I don't think they are lying. I mean it is possible we've got unidentified animals living up on the moors, and let's face it, there's plenty of space. But there are some round here that swear they've seen and heard the Hell hounds."

"Hell hounds?" echoed Jim, laughing. Brian's eyes glittered.

"You mean black dogs?" he asked.

The barman nodded. "That's right. The legend goes back hundreds of years, but there are some that swear they're seen the Devil's black dogs when they're been crossing the moors at night,"

"Get real!" Jim roared with laughter.

"What did they actually say they'd seen?" persisted Brian, ignoring his colleague's scepticism.

Steve leant forward conspiratorially. "Usually it's a big black beast with burning coals for eyes that appears in the lanes or fields, stares at them for a few seconds and then runs off, or simply vanishes. Some have said they've heard terrifying wild screams or baying that's scared them half to death."

"Foxes," muttered Jim, not impressed, but Steve shook his head.

"No. These folks know country sounds. Whatever it is that screams up there, ghost or flesh and blood, it's not a normal part of our countryside."

"What sort of people are we talking about?" asked Brian quietly.

"Farmers mostly," confided Steve, "but there have been others, a teacher, a policeman and even a visiting university professor, people that wouldn't have no cause to invent such stories. Stories that are likely to do them more harm than good if the word got out."

Tom shook his head in disbelief. "Ah, come on, I can accept there might be an odd escaped cat up there, but a ghost?"

"I agree," murmured Steve. "And stock has been killed. Killed and gone missing. Ghosts don't eat sheep."

Jim groaned. "Nothing might be eating sheep. There's always been losses on the moors. Animals wander off and die of natural causes. Plus the odd visits of rustlers and those, I believe, are on the increase."

"Rustlers wouldn't take an odd animal here and there." Brian pointed out. "They would take a lorry load."

Jim wasn't going to be convinced. "Dogs," he muttered. "They've always been a problem, especially now with so many townies coming out in search of the good life."

"I had a farmer in here a couple of days ago," said the barman quietly, "and it sure as hell wasn't no wandering dog that stripped his ewe clean. Just bare bones and a wool rug he found."

"Foxes and crows will strip a carcass," suggested Tom.

"Not in twenty-four hours, they won't, not a full-grown ewe," returned Steve darkly, and none of the others could think of a counter-argument.

"I'd like to talk to him," said Brian. "Would you have a quiet word? Tell him it's not for publication, just a personal chat off the record."

"I'll try, though I don't hold out much hope."

"All this fuss over a few bloody dogs," muttered Jim, but Brian chose to ignore him.

* * *

Next morning Brian arrived at the office later than usual, to find a note propped up on his computer.

Ring Mr Crabb. Re: puma.

He dialled the number, to be answered by Mrs Crabb's homely voice.

"Is it Mr Henderson speaking? Good, he wanted to have a chat with you. He's out with the tractor at the moment, I'll just call him, hold on."

He could hear her footsteps as they clattered across the stone floor. He remembered the Crabb's big comfortable old farmhouse. They were third generation farmers and the house wasn't the neat whitewashed thatched cottage so beloved of the tourists, but a lime-washed stone and cob building, the cobbled yard inches deep in a swamp of mud, straw and cow dung, through which numerous fowls scratched eagerly, splattering visitors with muck. Inside, the huge beamed kitchen was the centre of operations for both work and family life, the massive scrubbed and splintered pine table dominating the room, usually littered with dishes, farm accounts, newspapers and children's toys.

Hugh Crabb's broad Devon accent came on the phone.

"That you, Mister Henderson?"

"Yes. How are you Hugh?"

"Pretty well, thank you. A bit busy, mind, with the farm." He paused. "I thought I'd give you a call. It's about the beast my boy claims to have seen. I've been making enquiries myself and I've turned up one or two things that may be of interest to you. It seems that the boys aren't the only people to have seen the beast around here. I've also had a couple of 'phone calls from people that have read about the boys' sighting in your paper. Trouble is folks are keeping quiet. Especially after that government report on Bodmin Moor saying the beast there didn't exist. No one round here wants to be made to look a fool."

"Would any of them talk to me? There would be no publicity unless they agreed to it."

"I'll have a word with one or two. See what they say. One's a local farmer with a fair spread of land. He has seen a big cat on his place a few times."

"And he hasn't done anything about it?"

"Didn't ever see no reason to. Says as the beast's not done him any harm, so why should he harm it?" Brian couldn't fault the logic of the unknown farmer.

"Then he obviously hasn't lost any stock to the creature?" he asked.

"Seems, not. He were out lamping for foxes one night and he caught the cat full in the beam of his light. Reckons it were coming in answer to the squeaker so he's not too worried about it attacking his stock."

Brian was lost. He had no idea what a squeaker was, or why seeing the cat when hunting foxes had reassured the farmer that his livestock was safe. "I'm sorry, but perhaps you could explain that a little more to a poor ignorant townie. What's a squeaker?"

Hugh Crabb gave out a roar of laughter. "Sorry, Mr Henderson, I was forgetting you are unfamiliar with country ways. When you go lamping to shoot foxes, which to my mind is kinder than using snares or poison, we call up the beasts by imitating a rabbit screaming. There's some that use the old ways and can call up the foxes by mouth, but most nowadays have lost the art and they use a squeaker which is a sort of whistle that sounds like a dying rabbit. The fox hears the scream and thinks it's an easy meal so he's attracted to the sound. Then when he comes in range, we switch on the lamp and bang, one less fox to worry about. If the cat is attracted to the squeaker, it preys on rabbits like the fox, and as there's plenty of them around, it's got no need to look for other food."

Brian was far from sure that a big cat wouldn't eat a more varied menu. "But couldn't the cat attack prey other than rabbits?"

"Yes. However, judging by the size of the cat, the farmer reasoned that if it intended to kill stock, it would be taking more than just the odd chicken or lamb. Full size sheep and even cattle would be on its menu, and as they hadn't been, he assumed they wouldn't, if you take my meaning."

"It was as big as that?" asked Brian, horrified.

"Seems so. He reckons it were as big as calf."

"Was anyone with him?"

"His brother-in-law. I've spoken to him as well and he says the same thing."

"How good a look did they get of it?"

"Seems like it stayed in the torch beam for a good minute or so. It was very dark or black in colour and appeared to be fascinated by the light. It just stood there staring at them. They said its eyes glowed red, making it look real hellish."

Brian paused a moment and then spoke slowly. "This is important, Hugh. They definitely say it was black, not golden brown?"

"Yes."

"And they are quite sure it wasn't a dog?"

Hugh Crabb grunted. "They say it were a cat, and they are not the sort of blokes who'd say they've seen something when they haven't."

Brian hastened to ensure Hugh that he wasn't suggesting that the men were lying. "I'd like to meet them if it can be arranged," he added.

"I'll have words, Mr. Henderson, and see what I can do. Can you come over tonight? Say around eight, I'll try and have them both here."

"I'll see you at eight. And, many thanks. Oh, and Hugh, please call me Brian, I hate the Henderson tag."

Brian put the down the 'phone. All the witnesses said black except Amy Meakin who swore the animal she had seen had been brown like a lioness. Was Amy Meakin mistaken? After all, she had received a severe blow to the head? It was possible that she had mistaken black for dark brown. The woods where the accident happened were pretty gloomy, but there was something else that niggled him - the time. According to the boys, their encounter with the beast occurred around the same time as Amy Meakin's accident, yet the incidents were a good twelve miles apart. Could the same animal have been stalking the boys so soon after terrifying Amy's horse? It seemed unlikely, so could some of the witnesses be mistaken about the time, or even be lying? It was of course possible that someone, or everyone, had mistaken large dogs for something more unusual, but it was also possible that there were two different cats at large, both hunting in territory just twelve miles apart. And if the two were different sexes ...?

He sighed and stretched, then sorted through his pocket for change. It was time to tackle the temperamental monster and feed it good money in exchange for bad coffee.

CHAPTER 4

That evening, a few minutes before eight o'clock, Brian Henderson guided his car along the bumpy rutted track towards Crabb's farm. He guessed the gathering had been successfully organised by the collection of cars in the yard - a Suzuki jeep, two battered Landrovers and a small pickup, still loaded with bales of hay. Tucked away in a corner, in total contrast to the working mud spattered farm vehicles, he was surprised to see a clean white BMW. He parked his own car alongside it.

The front door opened as he crossed the yard, spilling out a miscellaneous assortment of barking yelping dogs and warm golden light. Hugh waited on the worn granite step to greet him, holding out a welcoming hand.

"Glad you could make it, Mr . . . Brian. I don't think you'll find it a waste of time."

"I'm sure I won't," Brian smiled as he stepped inside. He was surprised how crowded the kitchen was, it seemed at first glance as if faces and bodies were crushed and wedged in very available chair space. However, he was obviously the guest of honour for, at a click of their father's fingers, young John and his sister cleared a space at the table and presented him with what was obviously the best chair, a large highly polished old Windsor carver.

"Sit you down, Mr Henderson, and I'll pour you a cup of tea, or would you prefer coffee?" Mrs Crabb bustled around him.

"No tea will be fine," said Brian self-consciously, feeling the centre of attraction, though he didn't know whether it was because of his prestige as a newspaperman or simply because he was an outsider. He had a nasty feeling it was the latter.

Hugh made the introductions. "This here is Fred Tregown and his brother-in-law, Matt. They are the two I were telling you about that saw the beast when lamping, although Fred here has seen it on a number of occasions. This is my neighbour, Alan Parker. His land runs almost to High Torre. He's lost a few sheep on the moor. Found a couple of dead ponies recently that he thinks had been eaten." The men acknowledged Brian's greeting. "This here is Charlie Williams, known to one and all as trapper, for rather obvious reasons when you gets to know him like." Everyone roared with laughter as a small-wizened little man in a grubby tweed jacket and brown cloth cap eased himself forward and touched his brow with a dirt-encrusted hand.

"Evening, squire," he grunted and then slunk back into the anonymity of his dark corner, rather like a furtive animal unsure of territory.

"If you want to know anything about the goings on in the woods round here, you won't do no better than ask trapper, seeing as how he just about lives in them," chortled Fred Tregown.

"And if you fancies a bit of pheasant or maybe a nice piece of venison for your Sunday dinner, then trapper here's the man to see. Sort of falls over such things, he does," added Matt. Everyone, Brian included, roared with laughter. Trapper was almost a legend in the area, no one knew much about him, only that he lived in a remote place somewhere out on the moors, but he and his two dogs were a well-known sight around the local pubs. Ask Trapper to get you a moose and he'd turn up next day with two draped over his shoulders was the local joke and certainly, over the years he'd provided the meat for a number of local tables. When Trapper was drinking in a pub, said the local wits, it was pheasant not chicken in the basket.

"And this young lady is Miss Forsythe," continued Hugh, drawing Brian's attention for the first time to an attractive young woman seated in deep chair by the Rayburn.

"Jill," she said with dazzling smile, holding out her hand. Brian stood up to meet her and shook her hand.

"Brian Henderson," He introduced himself.

"I know," She laughed. "Your name has been rather bandied about in your absence."

He grinned back. "All bad, I've no doubt."

She shook her head. "Not at all. Seems you've made quite a hit in our little community." He watched as her long silken hair flowed around her shoulders with the movement, her eyes sparkled with health and vitality, sky blue with thick brown lashes. Her skin was tanned, her mouth wide and generous, revealing strong white teeth, her nose tilted, her cheekbones strong and high, giving her the classic English rose beauty. Definitely his type.

"I can't think how," he commented modestly, enjoying just watching her.

"Well, you've treated us seriously, not like upcountry folk. You accepted what the boys said without acting as though they must either be fools or liars," said Hugh gruffly.

"That's because I believed what they claimed to have seen."

"Yes, well, we have brought up our youngsters to tell the truth," said Mrs Crabb proudly, "so we know that if John says he saw something, then he did. But outsiders don't always understand our ways - the R.S.P.C.A. bloke for instance. He acted as though the boys were lying just because as he didn't see it, then it couldn't be there was his reasoning."

"Something's been killing my stock," muttered Alan Parker. "According to that prat, they'd all committed suicide."

Brian turned back to the young woman. "Have you seen it?"

"No, but I've good reason to believe it's there from what I've seen during my work."

"Which is?" asked Brian curiously.

"I'm sorry," interrupted Hugh, "I thought I'd told you. Miss Forsythe is our local vet."

"One of them," Jill explained. "I really can't claim to administer to the veterinary needs of this community single handed, I have two male partners and I'm afraid I am the junior of the practice."

"And you have reason to believe in the existence of a big wild cat?"

She nodded. "Sometimes farmers like Alan here, call me in to examine dead stock to try to determine the cause of death. Well over the last two years that I've been in practice here, I've examined a number of carcasses, and the results were rather startling, considering what wildlife is supposed to roam our countryside."

"You think they were killed by a big cat?"

"Certainly the kills were consistent with an attack by a cat-type predator."

Mrs. Crab handed Brian a cup. He stirred his tea and settled back in the big old chair. It looked like being very interesting evening and not just because he fancied the local vet.

Hugh looked at Brian and cleared his throat. Normally a quiet man, he felt very self-conscious as the centre of attention.

"You all know of course what our John and the other lads saw, so I don't think we need go into all that again," he began, ignoring the disappointed expression on his son's face. "Now I think Trapper's story is something that will interest you. Trapper lives out on the moors and there's not much goes on hereabouts that escapes Trapper."

"Or the attention of his dogs," quipped one of the other men. All eyes turned on Trapper, who shrunk back against the wall as though trying to dissolve into the plaster. A muddy looking lurcher peered out from between his master's feet and a scruffy terrier, which appeared to share some claim to ancestry with Jack Russell, was seated on the old man's lap.

"Tell Mister Henderson about your experiences," encouraged Hugh.

Trapper reached into a baggy threadbare pocket, producing a worn and evil-smelling pipe. "I don't know much about town and city folk," said the old man slowly as he lit the pipe. "I'm only used to country ways, so you will have to forgive me if I speak plain, mister, and tells it the way I sees it." He puffed thoughtfully, as if trying to sort out the words in his head. "Fact is, I ain't exactly one for conversation like, not really having much need of it."

"Please," said Brian, "tell it whichever way you find easiest."

Trapper sighed, "Well, let me say first - and I think there's few around these parts would dispute it like - I know this area and the creatures in it like the back of my own hand."

The others all nodded agreement. "He does that," muttered Matt. "No one round here knows it better."

"I've lived in the wilds all my life, man and boy. I didn't have any real education. My pa didn't hold with any schooling. He said knowing how to snare and skin a rabbit was of far more use to the likes of us than any book learning. So he reared me in the old ways of his people." He paused.

"His people?" Brian was totally captivated by the old man.

"A traveller, he was. Not like these long-haired hippies you see on the road these days, but a true gypsy. Anyway, he brought me up in these parts to know the countryside. I may not be able to read my letters, but there's not much I don't see."

"So tell us what you've seen Trapper," promoted Fred. "Tell the man about the beast."

Trapper drew slowly on his glowing pipe. "It were many years back when I first seen the signs like, signs that I couldn't give no name to. A shadow, padding through the woods at night, a creature that moved silently. I didn't ever see it clearly, just a glimpse of a dark shape, but come morning, it left tracks that were like nothing I'd ever seen." He stared at the swirling smoke spiralling upwards from his pipe. "They were very large, big as the biggest dog I've ever seen, the size of my hand, they was." He held up a brown dirty hand with broken nails to illustrate his point. "But the funny thing was, they weren't nothing like a dog, although they clearly showed deep claw marks; they were much more like a huge cat's print than a dog's. I ain't ever seen the tracks of a lion or tiger, but I should think they were pretty much like those I was seeing." He turned towards Jill. "Well, lady, you're a vet, right?"

She nodded. "Right."

"Well, let me ask you this, lady. How long does a dog live?"

"A well cared for dog, maybe fourteen to sixteen years on average. A great deal depends on the breed."

"Does a big dog live longer than a small one?" asked Trapper quietly.

Jill shook her head. "No. Quite the opposite. Big dogs generally have a shorter lifespan. A great dane for instance averages a life of nine to ten years, though a number don't even make that. Your little dog here," she gestured to the scruffy animal curled on the old man's lap, twitching, and whimpering as it raced after imaginary rabbits, "now, he should make fifteen or even more."

Trapper smiled and fondled the sleeping dog. "Well, I'll tell you something, lady, something that all your book learning won't explain any more than my own schooling. I've been tracking that there animal for well nigh fifty years." He chewed the end of his pipe.

"How do you know it's the same animal?" asked Brian. "It could be different dogs."

"I'm not sure," muttered the old poacher, sucking noisily on his pipe stem. "But it is no dog, whatever it is. I know a dog's foot and this one is different. If it's not the same animal, it's the same type of creature, and a creature that don't rest by no-one's fireside. All this talk of beasts. Some fools saying there's no such thing." He shook his head. "They know nothing. They don't know what haunts the darkness. My pa swore as once he saw the beast, but I haven't ever seen anything that I could put a name to."

"What did your father say he saw?" asked Brian.

"I can't rightly tell you what he saw, not seeing it myself like," answered Trapper with a frustrating honesty that one felt might have stemmed from his straightforward upbringing, but was more likely to have come from a cursory knowledge of the language of lawyers, gleaned from numerous minor skirmishes with the law and involving court appearances.

"But what did he describe?"

Trapper puffed leisurely on the blackened briar. "He swore till the day he died, that he had encountered the devil's own hound of hell up there in the moors."

"A what?" asked Jill.

"A devil hound," Brian explained in a whisper. "The whole country has legends of ghostly black dogs or Devil's hounds as they are sometimes called. They are supposed to haunt lonely places like the moors."

"A sort of hound of the Baskervilles?" she muttered trying not to giggle.

"Exactly! One of the legends was used as a basis for the story." He turned back to Trapper who was leaning back puffing contentedly. "Did your father describe the creature to you?"

Trapper removed his pipe from his mouth and tapped it out against the side of his boot before tucking it back into his pocket, so explaining the scorch marks on the threadbare tweed.

"He did that, many a time. Said the beast was sort of burned into his brain like, so he could never forget it."

"Can you remember what he told you?" asked Jill.

"Well my pa wasn't much more than a boy when it happened. He never could say exactly how old he was 'cause he didn't know his own age like, same as me. But he was a young'un, 'bout nineteen or twenty. There-abouts, anyway. It was late at night and he was out for stroll in the woods." The old man grinned wickedly.

"Bit of poaching, no doubt," laughed Matt. Trapper looked across at him with an expression of injured dignity.

"Course, if you've just asked me here to insult my poor old dead pa?" he began before Fred interrupted.

"Be quiet, man," he hissed at his brother-in-law.

Trapper ignored them both. "Like I said, he was out for a stroll, enjoying the night air and, unlike some as I could mention, minding his own business," he stared pointedly at Matt, "when he heard something moving through the undergrowth ahead of him. Something big like, but the sound wasn't right for a deer. You see a deer is long-legged and moves tall like, it treads dainty on the ground and the noise comes from its body moving high in the bushes, so the sound it makes is chest high, if you gets my meaning?" His question was directed at Jill and Brian, indicating that he took it as read that the others were experienced in the tracking of deer.

"But this creature wasn't making elevated sounds?" prompted Brian.

Trapper shook his head. "Not according to my old pa," he said. "He always said it was low, like a large body pushing through the undergrowth, maybe a foot to a foot-an'-a half above the ground. Like a badger, only bigger and heavier. My pa, curious like, stops and crouches in the thicket an' he stays there, quiet as a hunting fox, waiting. Suddenly everything was all clear as daylight. Whatever it is gets closer to the other side of the clearing and my pa sees the bushes moving. Then the beast comes out an' crosses the open ground in front of him." He paused, his listeners hanging on to his words with bated breath.

"What did he see?" asked Jill in a hushed voice that was almost a whisper.

"He said it were a big black animal, nearly as big as a calf but with a long body and powerful legs. It moved across the clearing slowly, almost like it knew it was being watched, and then it paused and turned to look at him. He said it had eyes that glowed like burning coals. Then it opened its mouth and snarled at him. He could see its huge white teeth, like something out of the jaws of hell, he always said."

"What happened then?" asked Brian.

The old man sighed. "Nothing really 'cause my pa, well, he got such a fright, he passed out cold, he did, and when he comes round, it was almost dawn and there weren't nothing there, just an empty clearing."

"So he might have dreamt it all?" commented Brian.

"More likely it came out of a bottle from what I remember of your old man," joked Matt, and Fred shot him a warning glance.

"Could he have imagined it?" asked Jill.

Trapper shook his head. "Oh, he could have imagined it all right, same as maybe I'm imagining all of you here. But there weren't no way he was imagining the prints, for when he looked along the muddy bank in the clearing there were huge prints, prints just like those I've seen myself."

"But it couldn't be the same animal!" exclaimed Brian. "If your father was a young man, then it must have been . . . . ." he paused.

"Eighty years, or thereabouts." Trapper turned to Jill. "So lady, can your book-learning explain how that animal can still be walking around in these here woods after eighty years." He started defiantly at his listeners, daring them to doubt a word.

"But it can't be an eighty-year-old animal, cat or dog!" said Brian.

"Not unless it has the lifespan of an elephant," remarked Jill.

"Well now, that would all depend on whether it's an animal at all," muttered the old man darkly. Jill looked confused.

"Meaning?" asked Brian but Trapper just shrugged his bent shoulders and stared thoughtfully into space. It was Fred that answered.

"There's some in these parts that believe in the ghost dogs and the Devil hounds," he said. "Some people reckon they've seen them in the darkness."

"So we're back to ghost stories," Brian sighed.

"Maybe so," muttered Fred. "But there is often truth hidden in old tales."

"As we've reason to know," added Matt, scratching his nose thoughtfully and then looked at his brother-in-law. "Tell him what we saw."

Fred stretched his legs out towards the fire. "Well, we were out lamping for foxes some three years back. Up Brown Torre way it was, at about two in the morning. We'd bagged three large dog foxes and was about to call it a night, when we hears an animal moving towards us. Well, we wait, quiet like, until we judged the animal was out in the open and then Matt here throws the beam and I've got my finger on the trigger, all ready to blast the bastard to hell."

"The light comes on," said Matt, "and bugger me if it didn't show up this huge black creature just standing looking at us. Fair put the fear of God in me, it did."

"What did it look like?" asked Brian eagerly.

"That's the funny thing," Fred replied quickly. "I saw it but I don't know exactly what it looked like. Mind you, I didn't stay around to get closely acquainted, I took one look and that was enough, I went like the bloody clappers, I'm telling you!"

"He's not lying," laughed Matt, "and I wasn't far behind him"

"You didn't try to shoot it?" asked Brian.

"Shoot it!" exclaimed Fred. "No, I bloody didn't."

"He didn't remember his gun till he got back to the house," chortled Matt.

"I'm telling you it scared the shit out of both of us!"

"But you must have see something of what it looked like?" queried Jill impatiently.

"It's hard to explain," answered Matt quietly. "It somehow wasn't so much what we saw as what we felt. We talked about it afterwards and we both had been affected in the same way, a sort of blind panic, and without even thinking about it, we just bolted."

"It was like Trapper here was saying about his pa," Fred added, "that he passed out. Well, I've never been nearer in my life to fainting. If I hadn't run, I'm damn sure I would have gone out cold."

"But what did you see that made you so frightened?" asked Brian.

"I remember the eyes," said Fred softly. "I'll never forget them, they glowed, like firelight. It was the eyes we saw first. They were like twin torch beams as they reflected the light from the lamp, and it was the eyes that gave me the willies. It was like nothing I'd ever seen. I didn't really stop to look at the rest, I just legged it."

"What do you remember Matt?" asked Jill.

Matt paused before answering thoughtfully. "Same as Fred here, I remember the eyes burning, and it was big, bigger than a ewe for instance. It was powerfully built, a real heavy-looking beast, and a very dark colour. I felt an unexplained terror that makes no sense, and it sounds silly but I'm sure I tried to scream and nothing came out."

"Did the creature react at all to you?" asked Jill.

Fred frowned. "I seem to remember it opened its mouth and snarled, showing bloody great white teeth. There was a scream as well, but to be honest with you, I've never been sure if it was the beast that screamed or one of us."

"Are you sure it opened its mouth to snarl?" said Jill quickly, and Brian had a feeling he'd missed an important point.

"You bet it did," agreed Matt. "It opened its mouth and snarled because I remember looking at its teeth and thinking, Christ, it has seen us! I expected it to spring at us, then I turned to leg it."

"But you are certain it opened its mouth to snarl?" Jill persisted.

Fred nodded. "Yes. I could see right down its bloody throat, and I remember thinking I'd found out what a bleeding mouse felt like when a cat pounces."

Brian turned to Jill. "Why does it matter how it snarled?"

"As I see it," she responded, "we've either got a rogue dog or a big cat wandering around the moors and it's important to know which. If it was a dog, then it would snarl like any dog, whatever the breed, with its mouth closed and its lip curled to show its teeth." She looked around and gave a slight smile, "ghost or otherwise. However, a cat behaves in a very different way, and snarls with its mouth wide open. If Fred and Matt here are right, then it was a cat, not a dog that they saw."

"If it were a cat, then it were a big one!" exclaimed Fred. "It were damn near the size of a great dane!"

Alan Parker had been listening intently to the others. "I've seen the bastard from a distance," he said softly. "I've spotted it loping across the hillside on a couple of occasions during the day. It's big and jet black. I've never got close enough to say if it's a cat or dog, but the way it moves, it's a killer."

His words sent a chill through the gathering. They sat in worried silence drinking tea, and wondering exactly what stalked the darkness beyond the cottage wall. There was some attempt at small talk, but soon the meeting broke up.

Hugh saw his guests to the door. Trapper gave a wave and shuffled off into the darkness, his dogs trotting at his heels, all three seeming to melt into the shadows. Fred and Matt shook hands with Brian and he thanked them for taking the time to meet him.

"Trouble is, mate, even if we know it's a cat, it doesn't really help us get rid of the bugger, does it?" Fred shuffled his feet.

"And I for one don't fancy meeting up with the sod again," added Matt with feeling.

"It doesn't seem to be dangerous," said Jill reassuringly. "It obviously had a chance to have a go a couple of times, but it hasn't attacked anyone. If it is a puma, then it is not a danger to us. It might knock off a few sheep, but it won't attack a human unless cornered."

Matt took her hand and grinned. "I'll remember that, Miss Forsythe, and do my bloody best not to corner it."

The men crossed to their cars, waved their good-byes and drove off, leaving Brian and Jill standing with Hugh in the open doorway.

"Well, Brian, what do you make of it?" the farmer asked with a worried frown.

"If it's worth anything, I think you've definitely got a big cat around here."

Hugh was circumspect for a moment. "I've got to be honest and admit I never believed all the beast stories. Thought it was a bit of fun, but now. . ." He paused and sighed. "Trouble is, if we have, what the hell do we do about it?"

"God knows!" Brian said helplessly. "Hunt it down, I suppose, though in a way it seems a shame if the animal isn't dangerous."

Hugh looked at Jill. "I know what you say, Miss, and I'm sure you know more than me about these things, but it appears to be taking stock and to my mind, if it can take a ewe, it seems like it might take a child."

Jill took his arm comfortingly. "If it is a puma, then they are rather timid creatures and usually prey on deer and rabbits. Their lack of aggression towards humans is why they have often been kept as pets." She paused before adding thoughtfully, "Although there have been a few attacks on humans recorded in the U.S.A. Possibly due to a lack of their natural prey or even human encroachment into their territory."

Brian was glad he'd parked by the BMW as it allowed him to walk Jill to her car after they had said their good-byes to the others.

"Where are you from?" he asked with distinct lack of originality.

She smiled. "Do you mean where do I live now, or where did I live before I came here?"

He noted with pleasure that the smile extended from her mouth to her eyes. "Both, starting with where do you live now?"

"I've got a small cottage just up the road from here, about two miles."

He glanced pointedly at her hand. "Do you live alone?"

She laughed and shook her head. "Not exactly, I share the cottage with Rupert and Mike."

"Two blokes? Isn't that a bit crowded?"

"Sometimes." She grinned, seeing his expression. "Especially in bed." Brian looked so shocked that she added quickly, "Mike is my great dane and Rupert is a rather battered old tom cat that I sort of adopted, or rather he adopted me."

"Is there a man in your life?" The walk across the yard was too short for any attempt to be subtle.

"You don't waste time on a lot of small talk, do you?"

They had reached the parked cars.

"Time wasted is time that could have been put to better use, as my old grandpa used to say." He grinned. "Now, to save you asking, I'll tell you all about myself."

"Was I going to ask?"

"I'm going to tell you anyway, potted autobiography coming up. Age? Old enough, but not too old. Married – once, all over: involved not: and interested in you, definitely."

"How about hobbies and job prospects?" asked Jill, slightly taken aback by the speed things were going.

"Job prospects, a gold watch, plated mind, not solid. Hobbies? Chatting up beautiful blue-eyed vets."

"Do you know many blue-eyed vets?" she said with a smile.

"Only one, so far. My hobbies are very restricted," he joked, then added, "Seriously, can we meet to discuss this business of the cat? How about lunch tomorrow?"

She shook her head. "Sorry. I'm on call over the next couple of days."

"Well, when then?" he persisted.

"Suppose I give you a ring when I'm free? I'll call you at your office."

Brian grinned ruefully. "Is that the brush off?" he asked as Jill unlocked her car.

"No. I really am up to my eyes in work at the moment, but I'll ring you in a couple of days. Besides, I'd like to do a bit of research on pumas before I see you again. After all, big cats are not exactly my field." She got into her car and started up the engine.

"Will you ring me if you get called to another kill?" he asked. "I'd like to have a look at one."

"Of course," she promised.

Brian watched her go. It had proved an interesting and disturbing evening. As he drove home through the darkness, he realised it was the time of night when hunting predators would be out and about. He wondered, with a shiver, just what the surrounding blackness hid. He was grateful for the security of the car as he sped home across the windswept moors.

CHAPTER 5

The following morning Brian ambled, bleary-eyed, into the office to face another day's long slog on the 'hatch, match and dispatch' routine, vaguely acknowledging Jim's greeting, as he trundled through the central office.

When he opened the door of the cupboard he was obliged to call his office, the telephone was already ringing. He looked wearily at his watch, surprised.

'Phones seldom shrilled at the *Exeter Times* before half past ten at the earliest, possibly, because no one ever expected the staff to arrive before that time. He lifted the receiver, cutting off its impatient trill.

"*Exeter Times*. Henderson speaking," he muttered, fumbling with one hand for a pencil and pad among the litter on his desk.

"Brian, Jill Forsythe here. I must talk with you."

He woke up at the sound of her voice and threw himself into his chair, wrapping the 'phone lead round his finger. "I always said that once I've been near a beautiful woman, she can't keep away," he said laughing. "Mind you, it's never happened before."

"Shut up, Brian, this is serious," said Jill shortly. "I must talk to you."

"You want my body?" he suggested hopefully.

"Brian, listen to me! The cat can't be a puma, it must be a leopard."

Her tone alerted him to the importance of the information, although he did not understand why.

"So?" To Brian a big cat was a big cat, regardless of species.

"If the witnesses are telling the truth, it is either a hoax or a leopard that's wandering around."

There was fear in her voice and he knew she was serious.

"I'm sure it's not a hoax," he said thoughtfully.

"Then we've got a real problem because we've got a leopard on the loose."

"What difference does it make?" he asked quietly. "A puma, a leopard, or a black panther, surely all that matters is that it's a big cat?"

"A hell of a lot! You remember what I told Hugh Crabb last night, that a puma was non-aggressive to humans and generally wouldn't attack anyone?"

"Yes, of course. You cheered the poor bloke up no end. I think he'd secretly been scared to walk across his fields."

"Well, he's got good reason to be."

"Why?" Brian was beginning to feel her panic.

"Look, I can't talk now. Can we meet for lunch?"

"Today? I thought you were busy?"

"I am, but believe me, this takes priority over anything else that might come up. The farmers can afford to lose the odd sheep, but they can't afford to have a feral leopard roaming around, whether black or spotted."

"Feral?"

"I'll explain when I see you," she said. "I've got to go now."

"Okay, don't panic," said Brian calmly. "I'll meet you in the Fox at one."

"No. Make it somewhere quieter, so we can talk. You know that little café opposite the pub? *The Kettle*. I'll meet you there."

"Fine. At one" He paused and added softly, "Jill, don't mention this to anyone else." He wanted to keep his story exclusive.

"Of course not," she said, her voice a little calmer, but the reason for her silence was different. "Whatever happens, we don't want to start a panic."

The 'phone clicked as she rang off. Brian replaced the receiver thoughtfully and stared at his pad. She had not even said goodbye. He looked up the 'phone book and dialled a number.

"Exeter Museum," trilled an operator-style voice. Brian sometimes thought that there must be a special training centre for switchboard personnel that taught the bland mechanical tones. "Can I speak to someone in the Natural History section?" he asked.

"Just one moment, I'll see if anyone's in," trilled the voice. He wondered if she talked like that at home. If she did, he decided, it must grate like hell on her husband's nerves. Still, at least he was spared the horror of electronic music." I'm putting you through," squealed the voice on an even higher note.

"Dr Smithson here, can I help you?" The voice was young, male and earnest.

"*Exeter Times* here, Henderson speaking." He paused trying to work out how to word his request. "Could you help me with some information please?"

"If I can, and providing it's not about my sex life," said Smithson cheerfully. "What's it like working for the local rag?"

"Er, fine," said Brian, rather thrown by the question.

"Fancied it myself at one time, instead of which I ended up in the stuff and pickle factory. Still mustn't grumble, it's a living. Well, for me anyway, if not for my clients," chuckled Smithson. "So how can I help the gentlemen of the press?"

"I'm researching an article on the consequences of the 1976 Dangerous Wild Animals Act," Brian explained. "You know the sort of thing: did people really go rushing out to release unwanted wild animals all over our countryside, and if they did, what happened to the beasts?"

"More animals have escaped from farms than as a result of the Act," said Smithson. "Though I've no doubt a few furry friends have been dropped by the wayside."

Brian took a deep breath. "Could a big cat, for instance, survive in our countryside?"

"Oh, undoubtedly it could survive," said Smithson cheerily. "Good food supply, plenty of cover and a reasonable climate. No problems at all."

"Do you think any are living in the wild?" Brian tried to keep the anxiety out of his voice.

"Hmm, that's a difficult one. A lot of people expected the countryside to be crawling with various unwanted beasties, but it just didn't seem to happen, and owners behaved in a rather more responsible manner than was anticipated. Of course the zoos were overwhelmed with gifts and finally had to shut their gates, so unfortunately a number of animals ended up getting the chop."

"So you don't think any were released?"

"Oh, I wouldn't say that. It's more likely that we've had a few loners wandering around quite happily without bothering anyone. In fact a puma was trapped a few years ago near Inverness, but in the main, our countryside is more likely to be cluttered up with escapees rather than deliberate releases."

"Even big cats?"

"A lot of people have tried to follow the trail of one of our fabled west country beasts, but so far, no one has come up with any proof they are really out there. The Bodmin beast took on the Ministry of Agriculture, the Exmoor beast saw off the marines. Cats are clever, but I'm not sure they are that clever."

"You don't believe there could be big cats on the moor then?"

"Everything is possible, old chap." Smithson paused. "Aspinal's Zoo lost a clouded leopard for about nine months until in the end a farmer shot the poor bugger. That's on record, but most escaped big cats are so tame, they just wander up to the nearest human, like a lost dog, looking for help. It's a mistake to suppose that caged animals are desperate for their freedom, you know. Quite the opposite. Most, if they get out, have a quick walk round, then head for home and the security of life behind bars. Some wolves escaped from a wildlife park in Wales a few years ago and the poor sods were shot trying to get back to their enclosure."

"So if a big cat did escape and survive in the wild, it wouldn't be a danger to humans?" asked Brian relieved.

"Highly unlikely," said Smithson. "The most popular big cat kept as a pet was a puma. That would be my bet if an exotic cat is roaming around. They are pretty harmless, unless you happen to resemble dinner, of course,"

"And man doesn't resemble dinner?"

"To a puma, no, not usually. Now if by any chance you had a leopard on the loose, then that would be a very different matter," said Smithson suddenly serious. "I for one wouldn't go walkies in the wood."

"So a leopard would be the most dangerous cat?"

There was a pause while he considered the question. "I wouldn't say it's the most dangerous, I think the tiger would deserve that distinction, and certainly lions have been known to acquire a taste for human dinners, but a leopard would be third on the list."

Brian could now understand only too well the reason for his early morning call. "So it's safe to assume a leopard living wild in this country could pose a threat to the local inhabitants?"

Smithson laughed. "It wouldn't do a lot for the local farm stock either. A favourite meal is goat. They will travel miles to attack them, and no doubt sheep would provide a suitable substitute. But rest assured, I'm quite sure the countryside is not about to be overrun with feral leopards."

"How can you be sure? You said yourself that we could have a few loners around."

"Cats, yes," replied Smithson confidently. "Remember we have native wildcats in Scotland. The odd puma or even a lynx or two could survive without problems, but not leopards."

"How can you be so sure?" persisted Brian.

Smithson gave a throaty chuckle. "Easy, old boy, if a leopard was on the loose for any length of time, then someone would have come up against it. And since we haven't had any reports of hikers or foresters ending up wedged half-eaten up a tree, then it's fairly safe to assume that all our British leopards are safely tucked up behind bars."

"Up a tree?"

"A leopard trait, that. Very tidy eaters, are leopards, with their own dining tables. They usually lug their prey up trees, quite a feat, so they can dine at leisure. Amazing really, they can carry up to twice their own weight up as high as sixty feet, just to keep scavengers away from the remains of their kill. Like us locking up the deep freeze."

Brian shuddered at the prospect. "Well, thanks for your help."

"Anytime. Sorry to put a downer on your story."

"Sorry?"

"Let's face it, old boy. A leopard running loose would make more exciting copy than one behind bars."

"I suppose so," murmured Brian, and Dr Smithson could be forgiven for totally misreading the reason for his lack of enthusiasm.

"Well, nice to chat to you old boy. In my job most of the characters I deal with don't make a lot of conversation. Ah, well, back to the dissecting table."

Brian thanked him and replaced the 'phone thoughtfully. He had begun to understand Jill Forsythe's sense of urgency. His own increased throughout the morning and it was with relief that he headed for their meeting place at lunchtime. He hoped she would provide more reassurance about the possible situation than Smithson.

She hadn't arrived when Brian entered the café, so he chose a table near the window to watch for her, and within a few minutes he spotted her car pulling into the parking space. If he harboured any idea that Jill had changed her mind about the identity of the beast, one look at her face when she walked in the door didn't give him a lot of hope on that score. She appeared to have aged overnight. Her face was drawn, her eyes pink rimmed as though deprived of sleep and her wide, generous sensual mouth was turned down, at the corners. He stood up and pulled out a chair.

"I think you'd better sit down," he said quietly. "You look like hell."

"Thanks. I feel like I look, but it's nice to receive compliments."

"What will you have to eat?"

Jill shook her head. "Nothing thanks, I couldn't eat. I'll just have a coffee for the moment."

"Nonsense. A working girl needs her calories," Brian grinned, but she failed to respond. "How about an omelette, I believe they do a good Spanish?"

She nodded. "I'll not promise to eat it."

Brian ordered and they sat in silence as the waitress brought over the coffee.

"Sugar?" Brian asked, more to break the silence than anything else. She shook her head. "Come on, cheer up. It might never happen!" He laughed and detected the strain in his own voice.

"I think it already has. I'm telling you, Brian, it has to be a leopard wandering around out there, and have you any idea what that could mean?"

"Some. I did a bit of research myself, after your 'phone call, I had a talk with a guy called Smithson at the museum and he pretty well put me in the picture. Thing is, why are you so convinced it's a leopard,"

Jill shivered slightly. "The colour. All that talk about the Devil hounds, everyone at the farm last night agreed that the animal was black or very dark, right?"

"Right."

"Well, I can't find any record of there being a black puma in captivity. They range in colour from tawny to fawn, so it would be a very rare and valuable animal, and there would have been zoological records. Leopards on the other hand are frequently melanistic"

Brian raised an eyebrow, "Sorry, you've lost me. What's melanistic?"

"It simply means a black colour morph. A melanistic animal is one born with a black coat colour. Like an albino is white."

"What about a panther? You get black panthers," responded Brian.

"Exactly. And a black panther is simply a melanistic leopard. It isn't a separate species."

"Aren't there any other big cats it could be?"

Jill shook her head. "None that improves the situation. The South American big cat, the jaguar, could answer the description, but it is just as dangerous."

"So we are in a no-win situation?"

"If there is a big black cat out there, I'm afraid so."

Neither found their appetite as they stared gloomily at their plates.

All they could hope was the witnesses were wrong.

That afternoon Brian made a call to Exeter police station, but if he had hoped for an offer of help, he had misjudged the situation. His call was put through to a friend of P.C. George Wells, the officer who received daily bulletins about Mrs Briant's black panther.

"I would like to discuss a rather difficult situation off the record."

"Can you give me some idea of the nature of the complaint, sir?" asked the male voice politely.

Brian let his pen slide across the paper in front of him, absentmindedly drawing a rather crude cat. "Well, it's a bit difficult. I work for a paper and I've got some information that I don't want to make public for fear of causing panic."

"I see sir. Well if you could just outline the problem, I'll see how we can help."

Brian took a deep breath. "Well I believe there is a leopard living wild on the moor." He waited for the startled reaction, which he failed to get.

"A leopard living on the moor," repeated the voice calmly. "And are you the owner reporting it lost?"

"No, of course I'm not."

"You know the owner then, sir?" asked the voice in a rather bored tone.

"No, I don't know the owner," snapped Brian irritably, feeling the conversation was not going as expected.

"Have you seen the animal?"

"No, I haven't seen the bloody thing, and I don't want to!" he exclaimed angrily. "I've seen evidence of it and others have actually seen the beast."

"Old Mrs Briant again, I suppose," sighed the voice. "She's got you press lads at it now, has she?"
"Who the hell is Mrs Briant?" Brian exploded. "Look, all I want to do is to take steps for the bloody thing to be trapped or shot before it kills someone. It's not lost, it's wild and it's not a pretty little pussy. This thing is big and it's a killer!"

"Are you reporting that it has attacked and killed someone?"

"No, but it bloody soon will!" exclaimed Brian "It has frightened some kids and some locals already, put one lady in hospital just a few days ago."

The voice suddenly sounded interested. "Put a lady in hospital, did it? Was she attacked?"

Brian sighed, already sensing failure. "Not exactly."

"Was she clawed or bitten?"

"No, just frightened."

"Then why was she in hospital?"

"She was injured falling off her horse."
"I see, sir. Because a lady fell of a horse, you believe we have a dangerous wild animal living up on the moors?"

"No. Not just because of that. Other people have seen it."

"But you haven't?"
"No," Brian sighed, accepting defeat. "I suppose it wouldn't help to ask you to ring the local vet who's examined a number of dead sheep?"

"No"

"I thought not."

"Well, I've recorded your complaint, sir, and if anything further develops, please do inform us and we will look into the situation. But really, as things stand, there is nothing we can do."

"I haven't made a complaint, I'm trying to warn you!" Brian threw his pen down with such force the plastic body snapped, splattering ink over everything. "For God's sake man, this thing could kill someone!"

"Yes, well, I've made a note of everything you've told me, sir, and I'm sure all the necessary steps will be taken to protect the public. Thank you for ringing us. Good day sir." There was a click followed by the dialling tone. Brian slammed the 'phone down in frustration.

"What do they want?" he shouted to the empty office. "A bloody body?"

CHAPTER SIX

I t was close to midnight before Trapper made his move. He lived in a derelict old shack in a tiny clearing in the woods about five miles from anywhere. Neither the local council nor the owners of the land knew about the shack, which was hardly surprising because anyone could pass within a few yards of the site without ever being aware of it, so carefully was it hidden by the surrounding trees. The cypress and pines provided height and cover, and the lower branches were walled in by dense thickets of holly and laurel, all planted years before by Trapper's father to provide a secure and safe hideout in the days when poachers were more than likely to spend long periods being entertained at one of His Majesty's hotels. To the casual passerby, it was just a thicket surrounding a clump of trees. The entrance was impossible to spot without being shown, and Trapper never showed anyone the small tunnel worn through the vegetation. He had to crawl on his belly for the first few feet, until the passage opened out rather like a path through a maze, and he could walk upright into the clearing. The trees were planted in a neat circle, the trunks straight and pruned, like the posts of a stockade. In the centre of the clearing there was a clutter of small sheds and a ramshackle shack built of timber and corrugated iron, just large enough to contain a small bed, a table, a kitchen chair and an old sink with a water tank overhead, kept filled by the rain. Alongside the sink was a cupboard in which Trapper kept his few possessions. A tiny wood-burning stove provided the old man with his heating and cooking facilities, and light came from an oil lamp, but this was seldom used, for on most nights Trapper was out working. His life was that of a nocturnal hunter and, like the animals around him, he slept during the day and prowled the forest silently in the darkness, his two dogs like shadows at his feet.

A creature of habit, like his neighbours the fox and the badger, Trapper made his move at the same time most nights, first to the nearest village pub where he wheeled and dealed, trading his previous night's hunting. He would sober up on the long walk home and by midnight he would again be slipping through the darkness that was his friend, the dogs moving silently at his heels, scenting the air for prey.

On this night, the moon rose high; a great silver disc with a pale frosty halo circling it, the cold light giving the shadows a deeper richer blackness and touching the treetops and grass blades with a frosty shimmer. The old man pulled his hat firmly down over his ears to muffle the cold, whistling his dogs to heel as he moved quietly forward, his shotgun cradled lovingly in his arms. His next move was always to check his traps of the night before. His first snare was empty, but the next three contained the hanging carcasses of unlucky rabbits, their limp mute bodies swinging from high wires, a trick to prevent the foxes from raiding the snares before Trapper could reach them. He bagged the chilled furry carcasses and reset the sprung snares, then moved on into the forest, towards the banks of the stream that splashed and gurgled its way from the open moors to cut its muddy path through the centre of the trees. It was the drinking source for all the animals, both the hunted and the hunters, and as Trapper knew from experience, it was the best place to watch for deer. He wasn't a see 'em and shoot 'em merchant. The old poacher was, in his way, a conservationist who would never kill anything but a young buck- - does were taboo because they were the future breeding stock and the older stags were tough. Bucks however, were expendable, and Trapper could cull their numbers without affecting the herd. He could kill without conscience and without crossing the wardens. The deer wardens of course noticed the yearly reductions of bucks and they had little doubt who was responsible, but they also knew that the old man would never overstep the mark. He was a professional, and as such he was respected by the other, more legal, professionals.

Trapper crouched in the undergrowth overlooking a wide muddy path where the stream splashed over rounded boulders and flowed across a shallow ford, which was both a crossing and drinking place for the deer. He cocked his gun and settled for the night's wait, his two dogs crouched watchfully and silently by his side. For the first hour everything was normal; two fallow does, their bellies swollen with young, moved cautiously out into the moonlight from the forest shadows, their heads raised, sniffing the air suspiciously. Trapper and the dogs didn't move a muscle, only their eyes gleamed brighter, revealing their alertness. The does were reassured and moved down to the stream where they bowed their heads gracefully and lapped up the freezing water, their sides heaving as they drank deeply, the moonlight touching their backs with silver. Trapper watched them with pleasure, despite his murderous intention. He loved the grace and beauty of the wild deer, just as he loved everything about his environment - the flowers, the birds, and the animals, even the quick dainty scurrying of the woodmouse, all gave him infinite pleasure.

A screech owl screamed from a nearby tree and Trapper became alert; it was a warning that danger was close. He guessed it was a passing fox engaged in its own hunting, but he couldn't move until he was certain. There was always the fear of human hunters, undisciplined weekend marksmen who endangered each other as often as the deer, and who shot and killed at random. He gestured his dogs forward into the undergrowth to flush out the cause of the disturbance. The two does jerked upright, scenting the danger, ears twitching. Suddenly, with a flash of white scut, they were gone, melting into the shadows, leaving only ripples in the water to mark their passage.

Above him on the ridge Trapper detected a heavy body moving through the undergrowth, the sound about waist high, too high for a fox or a badger but not high enough for a man. At once Trapper felt fear, something he was unaccustomed to feeling in the wild lonely places that were his familiar world. It wasn't even a fear that was easily understood, more a primitive instinct, a sixth sense that he had developed like an animal. He knew that whatever was out there was dangerous.

Then came the scream, a sound that made the sweat bead on his skin and the hairs on the back of his neck prickle. The frenzied barking of the dogs told him that they had found their quarry. He whistled back the animals urgently. Devil hound or big cat, he knew his dogs were no match for whatever was hidden in the darkness. But it was too late, the dogs had the scent of prey in their nostrils, the excitement of the chase in their blood and for the first time they were deaf to their masters calls.

Trapper abandoned his customary stealth. "Heel! Spike heel! Striker heel!" But the animals ignored the call; it was doubtful if over the din they could even have heard it. "Heel! Come on, heel!"

The crashing and snapping of branches indicated the direction of the chase, and whatever the dogs were pursuing, was about to break cover and cross the clearing. Heedless of his own safety, the old man started to run, frantically shouting for his dogs. Then everything seemed to happen in slow motion. From out of the darkness into the moonlit clearing bounded a huge jet black cat, the dogs snapping and lunging at its feet. Trapper froze in horror leaning against the trunk of a tree, panting.

The animal was at least the size of an Alsatian dog, but longer in the body and more powerfully built, it's short dark-haired coat gleaming in the silver light, highlighting the rippling muscles. Once in the open, the dogs circled out, growling and yapping, as the animal twisted to face its attackers. Trapper screamed for his dogs to come, but he remained unheard and unheeded. The dogs were enjoying the battle and were sensing a victory that trapper knew they could never have. He tried to sight his gun but was unable to fire for fear of hitting his own animals. He started on down the slope, ignoring the whiplash of the branches, but he was an old man and he slipped and stumbled just as the cat reared back on its haunches and lashed out with sharp blade-like claws. The lurcher screamed as the claws sliced across it, almost severing the head from its neck, a scream that wasn't repeated as the blood stained body was hurled aside. Then the cat turned its attention on the muddy faithful Jack Russell. The small dog had no chance; it had never before met such an onslaught of fury as teeth and claws rained about it. Yelping and bleeding, it tried to get away but the hunter had become the hunted and the cat sprang after it. Trapper heard the sickening crunch as the white curved fangs snapped shut on the tiny neck, the cat shaking the bloody body before flinging it aside to lie in a broken heap of torn flesh and fur.

Trapper gave a high keening wail, partly in anger but mainly mourning. His dogs were more than dogs to him; they were his friends, his family, his companions during the long dark nights. In those few seconds the old man lost everything that mattered to him. He also lost his reason. He aimed his gun and fired wildly. The shot peppered the beast which only served to infuriate it further. It turned its attention to its new attacker and sprang, its claws slicing through the old poachers arm, its teeth crunching into his leg, ripping cloth, bone and flesh. Strangely, he didn't feel the pain, only a white hot fury as he lashed back at the animal with the butt of his shotgun, feeling the jolt as it made contact with the side of the cat's head. The animal screamed and flinched away from the thing that hurt it, retreating from its new opponent. It disappeared into the darkness, the shelter of the forest and the night.

The old man lay sobbing and bleeding on the ground for a long time before finally struggling up and, using his gun as a crutch, he dragged himself to his feet and staggered painfully down to the clearing and the bodies of his beloved dogs. There was nothing he could do. Painfully, with his one good arm, he scratched a hole in the mud and dragged the two bodies across to lie side by side, covering them with earth and leaves, tears furrowing his mud-streaked cheeks. Then, exhausted, he half crawled and stumbled back through the woods to his thicket home. He was like a wild animal, and never thought to try to get help, although it was doubtful he could have reached anyone. Instead his instinct, like that of a wounded beast, was to go home. With his ebbing strength, he reached the site and crawled through the tunnel to the shack. That night, weak from shock and the loss of blood, he died. The cat had claimed its first human victim, though it was doubtful anyone would ever know.

Untended and unpruned, the trees gradually grew inwards over the years, burying the secrets of the shack in the clearing. It was the way Trapper would have wanted it. He belonged to the wild and had become part of it, had returned to nature, recycled into the trees that had once sheltered him. Locals in the villages and pubs noticed his absence over the weeks but no-one knew where he lived to check up on him, and most just thought he had moved on, one day to reappear, his dogs at his heels, a salmon in his bag, a brace of pheasant in his jacket. By the time people realised he was truly gone, he was already a part of the past, a tale told over a pint.

But Trapper left more than a memory; he left behind a wounded cat.

The beast crashed through the undergrowth for a distance until it was certain it was not being pursued and then limped to a halt, sitting to lick at the salty blood that trickled from its injuries. A hind leg dragged painfully, the bone fractured by the shot, its mouth was sore, and one eye had closed due to the blow from the gun butt. It lapped at the wounds and then circled, making a small hollow in the bushes where it settled to rest. At dawn, the big cat slept fitfully, tossing and jerking from pain. It was the first dawn that Mrs Briant failed to make her morning call to the police station. She didn't call because she had nothing to report, that morning there had been no visitor to her fishpond.

Unlike Trapper, the cat didn't die. It lay up for a few weeks as its leg knitted badly, the muscles shrinking, the injured limb gradually drawing up uselessly, leaving the cat just three sound limbs on which to run and hunt. It had another reason to remain hidden, for during the second week of its lying up, it gave birth to two cubs that sucked lustily at its sore belly.

The cat had to find easy prey to feed her family.

The deer moved silently through the trees, alert to danger but unable to resist the scent of the lush meadow grass beyond the trees. The cat lay stretched out along a branch, watching the russet backs pass beneath it. She was tempted, but any sudden movement sent stabs of pain through her body, making her reluctant to spring. She knew, without understanding why, that she was no longer a match for her normal prey. Even when a squirrel bounded across a branch above her, she hesitated, watching as the tiny animal, using the gnarled bark of the trunk for support, zigzagged its way towards the forest floor. Her eyes gleamed but her gaze was unblinking, the only movement, the gentle ripple of her flank as she breathed, outlining her ribs beneath her fur. The injury and motherhood had taken their toll and she was in poor condition, very thin, with her coat lacking its usual lustre.

The unsuspecting squirrel darted towards her, pausing frequently to nibble at the tender shoots of the branch tips. She licked her lips, her pink tongue curling across her teeth, anticipating an easy kill. Closer and closer came her intended prey. She waited.

Suddenly the squirrel froze; its small grey nose wrinkling as it sensed the danger. Spread-eagled as its delicate paws gripped the bark firmly, it hung suspended, its body arched, its tail rigid, tense as it tried to locate the source of its fear.

For a few moments, time seemed to stand still. The cat was in no position to attempt to strike out and the squirrel remained tantalisingly just out of reach of the outstretched paw. Neither animal was prepared to make a move. The squirrel could not see the cat but it was aware of a lurking menace, it knew a predator was near. It remained motionless, attempting to vanish into its surroundings, with every muscle prepared for instant flight once it had assessed the situation. It was an old male squirrel, having reached a mature age by always reacting to its instinct for danger. Young strong squirrels had come and gone, curiosity or bravado their downfall, but this animal always used stealth and caution. The dangers for a small animal were many in the wild, both from above and below. Foxes, badgers, mink, stoats and dogs hunted the ground; cats stalked the branches of the trees and birds of prey swept in from the sky. The squirrel had only speed and agility for defence. And its instinct for danger.

That instinct once again saved its life. It twitched its snub nose, its whiskers quivering as it picked up a strong musty scent, informing it that danger lay ahead. Slowly it began to retreat backwards, each paw lifted separately as it edged along the grooved bark of the trunk, ready for instant take-off, judging its moment perfectly. There was a flash of grey and it was gone, scurrying high into the slender leafy branches that could not support a heavy hunter.

The cat listened to the distant rustle of the leaves, marking the squirrel's departure. The need for stealth gone, she stretched, arching her back and stood up. Limping along the branch, she leapt down, wincing from the pain of her injured leg as she landed heavily on the ground. Like a shadow she belly-crawled through the grass to reach a hollow between the twisted roots of a large oak. As she pushed her head into the cave-like gap, she was greeted by a high-pitched mewing. The two cubs heard her coming and wriggled blindly towards her, scenting her warmth and milk. She gave them a quick inspection and a maternal lick, her rough tongue cleaning them before she stretched out to allow them to suckle. While the tiny crumpled black faces nuzzled her belly, she gave an involuntary purring growl, reassuring her cubs and also warning them not to take liberties. She was too sore to welcome an over-enthusiastic greedy greeting from her youngsters.

With the pressure of her milk eased, she gently pushed the cubs away with her nose, not wanting them to pull her about further. Ignoring the protesting squeaks, she washed them, cleaning the droplets of milk from their whiskers and combing through their soft fur, gently grooming them with her tongue. Soon they curled up, paws draped over swollen stomachs, satisfied and sleeping. She lay quietly for a while enjoying the peace, content with motherhood until she again felt the need for food. The cubs were taking nourishment that she had to replace and with a last nuzzle at the sleeping cubs, she left the den and, favouring her injured leg, limped through the wood to a sandy bank at the edge of a large field. She had to eat but her choice of prey was limited because of her disability. Rabbits scurried around a warren, nibbling the grass, appearing oblivious to the dangers that surrounded them. The food source was not sufficient to provide her with an adequate diet, yet the rabbits were plentiful and easy to catch. She was uncomfortable hunting in the open in daylight but her desperation made her accept the risks involved.

Before long she would have to find larger prey, but while the cubs were so small the rabbits would suffice.

A fox spotted her crossing his territory and bared his teeth in annoyance. Normally he would have retreated immediately, but the movements of the cat gave him courage as he recognised his enemy was disabled. Although he did not dare risk a challenge, neither was he prepared to retreat from the feeding ground. He crouched down and watched the cat slink across the rise to position herself above the warren. A slight growl rumbled at the back of his throat and his lip curled, revealing his sharp pointed teeth. If the cat heard, she ignored his defiance, her concentration focused on the rabbit burrows. She settled down to wait patiently for an unsuspecting animal to move into range. It was not a long wait.

The rabbit died instantly, it's back broken by the blow from her paw. She ripped the skin from the meat, using her tongue like a skinning knife, peeling the fur away from the muscle and crunching through the carcass. She felt better but not satisfied. Three more rabbits completed the morning menu before she limped back into the shelter of the trees, leaving the rest to the mercy of the watching fox.

The risk of spending so much time in the open was high for the prey involved. She had never been at a disadvantage before; food had always been easy to obtain. Perhaps a short wait on an overhanging branch till a fat helpless deer passed below. It was even simpler to stalk the sheep enclosed in the fields. The deer could break loose and run, but the sheep were captive and had nowhere to go.

Now, because of her injuries, when she had the most need for food, she had the least chance of getting it.

She lay up in a hollow for a while and cleaned her fur, licking her paws to wash her face like a household cat. Her jaw was healing quickly, only her crippled leg a lasting memorial to her encounter with Trapper's gun. She carefully cleaned the matted hair around the injury to her hip and gently massaged her leg with her tongue. It was less painful than it had been, but the muscles were tightening, pulling the limb upwards, making the leg useless. She was learning how to alter her gait, to run and walk on three legs. Soon she would be out of pain, but her speed and leaping power were seriously restricted. She had to eat and feed her growing cubs.

She had to find an easy prey.

She loped infirmly along the forest track, scenting the air, searching for any unusual smells that would suggest strangers in her territory. Deer, badger and fox scents she recognised and dismissed as of no importance. All were familiar, animals that lived and died around her, some lived in spite of her, others died because of her. All were part of her world.

She stopped suddenly and crouched low, her tail lashing from side to side as she sniffed. He was close. Very close. She gave a low growl that rumbled across the forest floor. He would know she was there but she had to assert herself, especially now. She scented his position and reared backwards, toppling sideways as she did so. She bared her teeth and snarled viciously. An answering snarl came from the bushes. A large dark brown male cat broke cover and ambled towards her, curling his lip and laying back his ears as he approached. She cowered down and pulled her head back in a throaty snarl, a mixture of servility and aggression towards her more powerful mate. He retaliated with a swipe from a heavily clawed paw, but it was a gesture rather than genuine anger and immediately he bent his head to touch her nose lightly with his. They exchanged their scent, gently rubbing chins in a motion rather like a human kiss.

He was the father of her cubs, but they seldom met during the year. While she kept to her own territory, seldom venturing beyond her familiar ground, he roamed across a much wider area, returning to her only when she called for him or, as now, when she knew better than to trust him, but she did accept the food he left when she was too heavy in cub to hunt easily. This year she had found his help vital and he had remained around for longer than usual, sensing that she had need of him.

Now that the cubs were growing and she was regaining her strength, he knew it was time to leave. No male stayed around a nursing mother, such an act was foolhardy and liable to end in serious injury for the more powerful cat. A female protecting her young was a formidable opponent.

He sniffed her rear end hopefully but accepted that he was out of luck. There was no point in remaining, she would scream for him when she next desired mating. Wherever he was, however many miles away, he would pick up her scent or hear her call. When they met again she would be ready for him. With a rumbling growl he flinched away from her striking front paw, which warned him not to attempt any liberties, and with a last snarl, he retreated backwards into the undergrowth.

She watched him leave with no emotion in her golden eyes. She felt neither sadness nor relief. It was simply the way of things. He would move on to pastures new and she would stay to feed, protect and teach their offspring. She would not see him until it was again the time for her calling. Then the cubs would be grown and independent of her, and the whole cycle of life would be repeated.

That was in the future; her pressing need now was to find food for herself and her family. For a while she could return to the rabbit warren, yet she knew it was not safe to keep going to the same killing ground. The experience of her encounter with Trapper had taught her fear for the first time in her life. There was always a slight danger when tackling large prey. A well-aimed kick or butt could do damage, a swing of a sharp antlered head stab into the attacker's body, even a fox or badger could turn and snap, ripping with sharp teeth at their assailant. These risks she was prepared for; she knew how to twist her body, how to dart in to make a kill without exposing any vulnerable part of herself. But her hunting skills had been useless when her injuries were caused by an invisible opponent. The pain had struck when she was out of reach of an attacker. She had not seen or smelt the aggressor, only felt the agony that came without any warning. She no longer felt secure in her own territory. For the first time, she had been the prey rather than the predator, and now she was uncertain of making a kill.

At the time when she most needed her strength and ability, she had lost both aswell as her confidence.

CHAPTER SEVEN

Andrew Roberts slung the canvas bag of newspapers over his shoulder and pushed his cycle along the kerb, stepping onto the pedal. "Are you going to band practice tonight?" yelled his best friend Matthew, just as he straddled the bike. Andrew acknowledged the question with a wave.

"You bet! I've been practising for weeks."

"Can I scrounge a lift? My dad's started lambing so he's a bit tied up."

"Sure," shouted Andrew as he started to pedal off. "We'll pick you up about seven. Okay?"

Andrew was thirteen, and being a village child, band practice and scouts were an important part of his life. City boys of his age would no doubt have grown out of such activities and be hanging around street corners, trying to appear old enough for bars and discos, but life in small rural communities like the moorland village of Shalton moved at a healthier and much slower pace. Vandalism existed but was more likely to entail nicking old tractor tyres from the silage heaps to make into swings than daubing graffiti or smashing up 'phones.

Andrew's parents didn't farm; they ran the local general purpose store and post office, and he delivered the evening papers to earn his pocket money.

His round was a long one, covering the best part of five miles to include a number of isolated farmhouses and cottages, but he knew the route well and would be home by five-thirty, giving him plenty of time for his tea and to get ready for band practice. Tonight they were auditioning for parts in the Easter concert. He'd driven his family mad for weeks with his constant practice, but it had been worth it, and he knew the choice of lead trumpet was between himself and David Webb. Andrew wanted the solo spot for himself; he'd worked hard, had even prayed at Sunday School to succeed, and although he was feeling nervous, he was reasonably confident that the coveted position would be his. He was eager to get home for a last quick blow before the audition.

He had one less house to deliver to as old Mrs Briant had been taken to hospital. He was sorry for the old lady, a nice old stick, who always had a cake or a biscuit for him and in summer would offer him a cold drink. Trouble was she talked non-stop and she was difficult to get away from. She was probably lonely, like his dad said, and would be better off in a home where she would have someone to talk to and people to look after her. Funny thing was that they'd not taken her to an old folk's home, as everyone expected, but to the big mental hospital twenty miles away. It didn't make sense. She did ramble on a bit about the past but she was certainly no loony. Still, it wasn't his problem, and without her to call on tonight, he could knock a good quarter of a mile off his route and get home that bit sooner.

He was almost through his round when he turned into the lane that cut through the woods to White Cross. The narrow road wound in tight bends, the trees crowding up to the fencing, trunks leaning over in some places so that the branches could link twiggy fingers with their companions opposite, making cool dark tunnels that in summer, when the trees were in leaf, completely blocked out the sun. But it wasn't summer as Andrew pedalled along; it was spring and the branches were just showing green. As the sun set over the hills, the hedgerows appeared ghostly with their froth of white blossoms, the grass verges dotted with clumps of pale primroses that gleamed in the twilight. His wheels crunched over the gravel of the drive of his last delivery as Mrs Pascoe came to the door to take the evening paper, warm light flooding from the hall into the dusk.

"Thank you young Andrew. Would you like to come in for a quick warm before you go back?" she asked cheerfully.

"No. Thanks, Mrs P. I'll be on my way. It's the auditions tonight for the Easter concert and I want to get back early."

Mrs Pascoe waved the paper at him. "Well, good luck for tonight, dear. What are your chances?"

Andrew grinned. "Quite good, I think," he answered, unworried by the lack of modesty. His father had always said, 'If you do a thing, do it well and don't be afraid to be proud of what you've done.' He did play well, so why should he not say so? With a last wave, he pedalled away down the drive. Mrs Pascoe had no idea, as she waved back, that she would be the last person on earth to see Andrew Roberts, for he would never reach his home or play in the band again. Andrew Roberts was cycling out of the light and out of life.

When her son still hadn't returned home at seven o'clock, Mrs Anne Roberts felt the first stirrings of alarm. She glanced at the kitchen clock.

"He should have been home by now," she said to her husband, who had just closed the shop. "His tea is ruined."

"Probably just stopped off for a chat along the way," suggested Dave Roberts, knowing his son and the boy's total lack of any sense of time.

"Not tonight, he wouldn't. It's the audition."

Dave Roberts sighed. "Give him a few more minutes, then if he hasn't turned up, I'll go and look for him. Give Matthew a ring. He might be over there."

But Andrew was not at Matthew's, nor at any of the houses on his round. Mrs Pascoe confirmed that he had intended going straight home when he left her.

"Something's happened to him, I know it has," said his worried mother.

"Don't panic," soothed her husband. "He's most likely had a puncture and is walking back. I'll take the car and go and meet him."

"Suppose he's been in an accident?"

"We'll cross that bridge if we come to it," said Dave grimly. "But I'm sure..." At that moment the 'phone rang. It was Mr Pascoe.

"Dave, I think you'd better get over here right away," he said quietly. "The police are on their way."

"What's happened?" asked Dave, his wife clinging to his arm.

"Hard to say but it looks like your son had an accident," replied Pascoe cautiously.

"Is he all right?" Dave tried to fight the sickening fear that was grabbing his innards in an iron grip.

"We don't know. Please just get over here quickly." Pascoe put down the 'phone abruptly.

To Dave Roberts, the call didn't make sense. Why didn't Pascoe know how Andrew was? Was the boy unconscious, or what?

"I'm going over there!" exclaimed Dave, slamming down the 'phone.

"Oh dear, God! What's wrong? He's been hurt?" cried his wife.

"They didn't say he'd been hurt, just asked me to go over. I expect he's smashed up the bike speeding to get back early."

"I'm coming with you."

Dave shook his head. "They didn't say he was there. I expect he's walking back and they want me to collect the bike. I'll probably pick him up on the road but you must say here in case I miss him. I'll ring you from the Pascoe's." Before she had time to argue, he was out of the door, leaving her sick with worry.

He did not see Andrew along the roads and as he turned his car into the lane leading to White Cross and the Pascoe's house, he was halted by a police stop sign, beyond which two police cars were parked, their lights flashing. As he pulled up, a policeman with a torch came out of the darkness.

"Evening, Sir. I'm afraid this lane is closed for the moment. Where are you going?"

"I'm Dave Roberts. I was told to come over to get my son."

"Your son would be Andrew Roberts, would he, sir?"

"Yes. For Christ's sake, tell me what's happened?" shouted Dave. "Has he had an accident or what?"

"What makes you think he's had an accident?" asked the policeman calmly.

"What the hell am I supposed to think? He hasn't come home, you're here and Pascoe told me to come over right away."

"Yes, well, we really don't know what has happened, sir, if anything. If you would like to leave your car here and come with me, the sergeant would like a word with you up at the house."

Dave leapt out of the car, leaving the keys in the ignition. "I think you should switch off your lights," said the policeman quietly.

Dave switched off with the uncomfortable feeling that the policeman was treating him with pity. As they walked up the lane, Dave was conscious of the lights flashing in the darkness of the surrounding woods, but his main attention was to the flash-lit group of figures in the lane ahead. He recognised Ted Pascoe, but the others were all uniformed policemen.

As they reached the gathering, the policeman escorting him said, "Mr Roberts, sir. The missing boy's father."

"Missing?" shouted Dave. "Will you kindly tell me what is going on?" Pascoe stepped forward and took his arm.

"Sorry Dave, I couldn't tell you anything on the 'phone, but it would seem Andrew has had some sort of accident in the lane." For the first time Dave noticed his son's bike lying across the lane, the empty paper bag a few feet away from it.

"Where is he?" Dave fought to remain in control of himself. It was like a nightmare, the floodlit darkness, torch beams dancing like fireflies in the trees and everyone refusing to tell him what was happening.

The sergeant smiled sympathetically. "Perhaps it would be better to go up to the house, sir. Then we'll explain what we know, which is precious little at the moment." He turned to Pascoe. "You don't mind if we use your place, sir?"

"Of course not. Come along, Dave, let's go and sit in the warm."

Almost like leading a child, he guided Dave up to the house, past the floodlights, past the tumbled cycle, past the numerous policemen that seemed to be everywhere.

In a dream-like state, Dave was soon seated in the Pascoe's kitchen, an untasted cup of tea clasped in his hand, listening to the sergeant's low tones.

"So you see sir, after your call to Mrs Pascoe, Mr Pascoe went out into the lane to see if your lad was anywhere around, thinking he might have met friends and be chatting, or perhaps had tumbled off his bike."

"And had he?" asked Dave numbly.

The sergeant sighed. "That's the point, sir, we just don't know. Mr Pascoe found the bike lying just as you've seen it, but we can't find Andrew. We don't know if he's had a bump on the head and gone wandering off into the countryside or whether he's walking home by a short cut and got lost. If he was simply walking home, we reckon he should have got there by now, even if he was limping. What is it? A mile or so? The fact that he hasn't reached home yet is obviously worrying"

"He must be lying hurt somewhere," cried Dave, leaping up and spilling the hot tea. "I must go and look for him!"

"We've plenty of men out looking," said the policeman soothingly.

"They are all well equipped for a night search, and they're trained for it. You will be better off back home with your wife in case he turns up there." Dave looked the sergeant directly in the eyes.

"But you don't think he will, do you? You think something dreadful has happened to him."

I'm sure he will turn up, but obviously something unusual has happened to him to alter his routine. However, we don't know yet what it is or whether it is serious."

"But you think it is?" persisted Dave, the hysteria evident in his voice.

"Now you and your wife can help by listing any places you think he might go to, friends, favourite play areas, anywhere he might have gone for help, or wandered to if in a confused state."

"I've already contacted his friends. No one has seen him."

"Would he have been afraid to come home for any reason? Had you rowed about anything?"

Dave shook his head in despair. "No. Nothing like that. He was looking forward to going out this evening. It was important to him."

The policeman smiled reassuringly. "Kids often go missing for a few hours. One always fears the worse, yet ninety-nine times out of a hundred, they turn up safe and well."

But they don't just leave their bikes dumped in the road."

The sergeant glanced at Ted Pascoe, before looking back at Dave. "No, not usually, sir," he said quietly.

The misery didn't end with the night. It carried on into the light of the following day. At two in the morning, Dave had insisted that Anne should go to bed after taking a sleeping tablet left by the doctor, but even then she hardly slept; it was as if her anxiety overwhelmed and smothered the effect of the sedative. Her eyes were shut but her mind was distressingly active. When she did sleep, she suffered nightmares that were not to go away with the dawn.

All day the Roberts' remained in the sanctuary of their home, waiting for news. Friends and neighbours called in briefly, offering help and sympathy, although most of the local men were out with the police, helping in the search of the surrounding countryside. Dave wanted to be with them, to be doing something physical in the search for his son, but he couldn't leave Anne. She was at breaking point, so he accepted the police reassurance that everything possible was being done and stayed by the 'phone, both dreading and hoping for it to ring with the news that Andrew had been found. It was the longest and most terrible day of their lives, and the darkness brought them no relief when the search had to be abandoned for the night. A policeman explained it was impossible for the searchers to cover the rough ground in the dark.

"He may be lying hurt somewhere, unable to get help," sobbed Anne bitterly. "They can't stop looking. They can't!"

But they had to. Two detectives arrived that evening to question the family about Andrew's friends, the places he went to, the people he knew. They wanted to know how he got to school, how he behaved at home, what was his relationship with his parents.

"It's always possible he's simply run away for some reason," explained one of the detectives, "You'd be surprised how many children do so without warning."

"Not Andrew," Dave said emphatically. "My son loved school, he was doing really well, and he was happy at home. He'd no reason to run away, none."

The school and the boy's friends confirmed his father's opinion.

The other detective sighed and put away his notebook. "On the face of it, I'm inclined to agree with you," he said grimly. "But we have to explore all possibilities before looking at the worst."

"And that is?" asked Dave, but the detective just shrugged.

"You will keep looking for him?" pleaded Anne tearfully.

The first detective patted her hand. "We'll not stop looking for him till we find him," he promised, and meant it, for no policeman ever became so hardened that he could face the mother of a missing child without feeling a mixture of pity and anger. Especially a child that in his heart of hearts he didn't expect to find alive.

Anne clung to his hand and gazed up at him, her eyes red and puffy, her cheeks streaked with tears. "Please, please bring him home to me," she sobbed bitterly. "Please bring him home."

* * *

Brian Henderson stared at the photographs littering his desk, trying to decide which ones were worth forwarding to the national papers.

"Nasty business," Tom Bates sat on the side of the desk and flipped through the pictures with a professional interest. Andrew Roberts beamed up at him, Andrew in his scout uniform, obviously camping, Andrew on holiday eating ice-cream, Andrew in his band uniform, playing football, climbing a tree. "They sure took a lot of photographs of the boy."

"They're that sort of family and he was an only child," Brian said grimly.

"Was?" said Tom with raised eyebrows.

Brian gestured helplessly. "Let's face facts. The kid seems to have no reason to leave home, he just wasn't the sort. The family aren't well off, just an ordinary family with a small business, not exactly ransom material. Yet the lad appears to have vanished off the face of the earth, and the police are at a loss."

"So definitely an abduction?"

"Looks like it."

Tom stared at a picture of Andrew smiling happily. "Heard they've brought the body dogs in," he said.

"A couple of days ago, but they've not turned up a thing. The search parties have scoured the area, police, troops and locals. There must have been a couple of thousand people altogether, but they've found nothing," Tom sighed. "I suppose it must have been a snatch, grabbing the kid off his bike and dragging him into a car, in which case the body could have been dumped anywhere from Cornwall to Scotland."

Brian nodded. "On the face of it, that must have happened, yet even so, there are one or two things that don't add up. The lane, for instance, is very narrow at that point, too narrow for a car to turn round, and the only way you could drive along it is to pass Ted Pascoe's house, yet it seems no one did that night. In fact the boy disappeared so close to their gate the Pascoe's swear blind that they would have heard the boy yell if he'd been attacked or knocked down. They weren't watching telly, and in their front room they can hear the traffic a quarter-of-a-mile away on the road. It's a local joke that if you go to visit them unexpectedly, by the time you reach the drive they've got the door open and the kettle on."

"And they heard nothing that night?"

"Apparently not, yet the conditions must have been good for sound because Mrs Pascoe actually heard Andrew coming with her newspaper and went to meet him."

"And he disappeared right outside the Pascoe's place? How about the Pascoes themselves? Anything know about them?"

"Both elderly and clean as fresh snow. No reason to suspect them of anything." Brian tossed a picture across to Tom. It showed Andrew's bike lying where it had been found, and in the distance could be seen the gates of the Pascoe house. "See anything odd about that picture?" he asked.

Tom studied the photograph intently, then shook his head. "Only that it is obvious the boy must have come off the bike suddenly, either knocked off or fallen."

"Well, if he'd been pulled off, say by someone waiting for him in the lane, then it would have been difficult to get the boy or his body the distance along the road to a parked car. We know from the results of the searches that he certainly hasn't been dumped close by."

"Then it has to be a snatch from a passing car," said Tom thoughtfully. "If we take it for granted that the lad didn't go off on his own accord."

"The bike lying in the road certainly doesn't suggest he went voluntarily and there doesn't appear to be anything in the boy's background to suggest he would run away. In fact, I think the police have ruled that out as a possibility."

"So it has to be that the Pascoes simply missed the car. It would be easy to do, even without the radio or television on. You'd only need the kettle boiling, the loo flushing, or just be talking."

Brian frowned. "No, I don't think so. I went up there as soon as the police opened the lane again and had a good look round myself. The ground was pretty soft, holding tyre tracks. Most, of course belonged to the police vehicles. If a strange car had driven down the lane, it would have left tracks, yet the police found nothing."

Tom remained silent for a moment. "They reckon that ninety-five per cent of crimes of violence are committed against people who know their attackers," he said thoughtfully. "Most are domestic, but others are neighbours or tradesmen, people you see every day."

"Look at this picture, at the position of the bike," said Brian.

"It does look as if the boy was knocked off. If he'd just got off and walked, he'd have propped up the bike against the hedge, not just slung it down like that."

"Not only that," said Brian. "Where it's lying. A car couldn't have passed without driving over it. A motorbike could have got round it, but that would have been noisy and left tracks. Also, a bike couldn't really have been used to move a dead or unconscious passenger, or someone captive against their will."

Tom stared at the photograph, screwing up his eyes in concentration, then he sighed and threw it down on the desk. "So what do you make of it? Or the boys in blue?"

"That it doesn't make any sense. If I believed in such things, I'd start wondering about flying saucers and time warps!"

Both men gazed down at the scattered photographs, Andrew Roberts grinning happily back at them.

"Oh, fuck it!" snapped Brian. "Let's go for a pint."

*　*　*

Exeter was buzzing with the story of the missing boy and the *Fox and Hounds* was packed to capacity. It was like a convention of media reporters for they had arrived like flies to a corpse at the first hint of the tragedy. Other people's misery or drama was their bread and butter, and if the story involved a missing child, well, it was the jam on the bread. The pub was a meeting place of friends and rivals, a beery reunion.

"Hi, Bob. You old bastard! Still with that fucking comic you call a paper?"

"Jesus wept! Steve. Don't tell me they've banned you from civilisation again!"

"See, I was down in Brighton like, covering this bloody boring conference, and when I got fed up, I just wandered down to the beach where there's all these lovelies sunning themselves, so I just showed them my card and told them I was talent spotting for page three."

"You crafty sod. Did it work?"

"Work? I'll tell you, mate, I've got enough dirty snaps on file to outdo Playboy! They couldn't wait to get back to my hotel room and strip off. It was better than those weeks in Saigon! And fucking cheaper!"

"Hey, Jeff. Over here! Thought you'd come crawling out of the woodwork. See this guy, saved my bleeding neck he did, when we were over the water. I'll tell you blokes, if it hadn't been for this idiot, I'd have been making the fucking news, not writing it!"

Brian leant on the bar and listened to the banter. He hated it, and hated them. Their conversation and constant references to the worlds trouble spots - Rwanda, Israel, Bosnia, Iraq, Afghanistan, Northern Ireland - it was the world he'd somehow missed, and they made him feel a hick, a country bumpkin.

"You the local man?" asked one London reporter, the contempt barely concealed in his voice. "Must be a change for you, having a bit of action around the place." Then he turned away, having done his bit to placate the local natives and returned to more interesting conversation with the real professionals.

Brian stared morosely into his beer. They were all on his patch; it was his story, but the papers would be filled with their copy, not his. He felt used and rejected, and what made it worse, they didn't even care about what had happened. It didn't matter a shit to them that just up the road was a grieving family, that a young boy was probably dead. Nothing mattered to them but getting a few lines in their respective rags, and cutting each other's throats in the process.

"Quite a circus, isn't it?" Tom was standing beside him, staring with ill-concealed contempt at the noisy crowd, cameras slung around necks, recorders over their shoulders and dog-eared pads sticking out of their pockets.

"I'll tell you what. I've not had the likes of this sort of trade, not in my time here." Steve Hockley beamed as he mopped up the spillage from the bar. "I've had to take on extra staff. They pour it down like it's going out of fashion."

"If this lot stay around in one place for any length of time," muttered Brian, glaring at the crowd, "it doesn't go out of fashion, it becomes extinct."

"At least one person is in his inky little heaven." Tom laughed as he pointed to Jim holding court, his status as an editor elevating him slightly from the common country herd. There wasn't a pressman in the pub who might not one day fancy retiring to a quiet country rag where he could live on past glories with no risks and a steady income.

"How long do you reckon this lot will hang around?" asked Dave.

"Until something better and dirtier turns up," said Brian bitterly. "Or until the boy is found. Whichever comes first."

Steve frowned. "It makes you wonder what the hell is happening to the world. Perverts that rape and kill kids. They should castrate the bastards and then top them."

Brian let the surrounding conversation float over his head, lost in his own thoughts. A leopard living, perhaps even breeding wild on the moors - it was a disturbing notion.

* * *

A few miles from the pub, a line of overall clad police officers, recruited from all over the southwest, were crawling along in slow painful progress across the rough ground. Every inch of the red Devon soil had to be checked by hand and eye. Each discarded sweet wrapper, windblown rag or chucked bottle or tin had to be collected and recorded before being put in black polythene sacks, and eventually passed to the rear of the creeping line. Even tiny objects, such as a lost button or used condom, representing past passionate moments beneath the trees, were kept and labelled for later analysis.

"I don't know about lover's lanes, I reckon this should be named Screw Woods," cracked one wit as he held aloft a torn rag identified as a pair of woman's knickers.

One policeman found a splintered piece of gleaming bone and debated whether to bag it.

"You'd better chuck it in," advised a colleague who was crawling beside him.

"They said everything, no matter what."

The policeman obediently bagged the bone, labelled it and passed it back.

"What's this? Your sodding lunch?" chortled the collector.

The bag containing the bone fragment was added to the growing pile of exhibits. Later it was eliminated as a possible clue, which was rather unfortunate because the chewed bone represented part of the mortal remains of young Andrew Roberts. A few pieces of bone and wind-blown shredded cloth was all that was left for the police to find. Unfortunately the searchers were unaware of this fact. The black cat settled quietly in the fork of a large ivy-festooned old oak and watched with bright un-winking amber eyes as the dark figures crawled beneath her. She stretched contentedly and felt the pull as one of her cubs suckled. She had fed well on an easy kill and was happy to lie up for a few more days before having to hunt again.

Had the police officers glanced up, they wouldn't have been able to detect her dark shape among the shadows of the tangled ivy. However no one even tried, for the search for Andrew was on the ground, not up in the trees.

The cat shifted slightly and washed the dozing cubs with a warm rasping tongue. She was disturbed by the unusual activity in the area but had no way of associating it with her own presence. Satisfied her young were clean and full, she snuggled down around them, providing a warm furry shelter. She closed her eyes and slept, unheeding of the voices and moving bodies below. When she awoke it was night and the humans were gone. The scent on the wind told her lambing had begun, and she knew that when she was hungry again, food would be there for the taking. Easy kills. Even for a lame cat.

CHAPTER EIGHT

No news is poor news. The mystery of the missing Roberts boy unsolved within three weeks, the last of the upcountry media merchants had headed towards pastures greener. The *Fox and Hounds* was again the quiet gathering place of a few locals and the staff of the *Exeter Times*. There had been no clues to suggest the whereabouts of Andrew Roberts. One policeman commented dramatically, it was as if the boy had been spirited away, carried off by a flying saucer. After hundreds of man hours, the police were no nearer a solution to the boy's disappearance than when Ted Pascoe first reported finding the bike.

The main topic of local interest was still Andrew's fate, but other matters had begun to creep into the conversation, matters of interest to the rural community. Only the Roberts' home was able to shut the rest of the world away. Unable to leave his wife in her distressed state, Dave Roberts arranged for someone from the village to take over the running of the shop. As the weeks became months, the Roberts quietly, and without fuss, moved away from the area and its memories. Mrs Roberts never recovered from the loss of her son, and spent the years hoping that every knock on the door or telephone ring was heralding his return.

"If he was dead, they would have found his body," she reasoned.

A new family with three children took over the business. It was noted by the locals, however, that none of the children delivered newspapers. Every evening their father rattled along the twisting lanes in his van, dropping off the newspapers on Andrew's old round.

As the boy's disappearance became old news and things returned to normal in the Times building, a spate of sheep killing was brought to Brian's notice. He quietly organised interviews with farmers alongside his assignments and kept his own records.

The results were surprising.

Almost nightly, over a wide area, lambs were simply vanishing. The farmers put their losses down to foraging foxes and attempted to dispose of the unwelcome visitors. Coping with the strenuous lambing period and patrolling the fields at night in an attempt to cut down the killer fox population left them stressed and tired. Yet, despite the increasing number of decaying russet corpses piled in the farmyards, the lamb losses continued on an ever increasing scale.

"Ain't never known nothing like it," complained Eric Pearce bitterly. "First I lose ewes to bloody dogs and now I lose my best lambs to sodding foxes! I'll tell you, this is a mug's game, and if it goes on much longer, I'll be out of bloody business."

"I suppose it definitely is foxes taking your lambs?" asked Brian.

"Has to be. One animal getting carried off at a time, that's not the way dogs behave. They don't do it for food. Just a bit of canine fun. A pair of dogs can leave thirty or forty dead or dying sheep within a few minutes. They chase them, you see, run them off their feet, snapping and biting at them." He paused thoughtfully. "Mind you, the trouble I had a while back, that wasn't usual, not the carcasses being eaten like that. Proper stripped to the bone. I ain't never seen the likes of that before."

"But you've not had that sort of trouble since?"

"It's hard to say like, whether I have or not," Eric said frowning. He pushed his cap back and scratched his balding head. "I've lost a couple of ewes, like, the same way as I've lost the lambs."

"How do you mean, lost? D'you mean you found them dead, or what?"

Eric shook his head, almost dislodging his worn cap, and stared thoughtfully down at his dung-caked boots. "I mean what I say. One day the buggers were in their field, the next day gone! Not a tuft of wool, nothing! Fair big ewes they were, one in lamb and about to drop."

"Could they have wandered anywhere?"

"I suppose so," agreed the farmer grudgingly. "They'd have had to jump over a four foot fence to do so - which though not impossible - is highly unlikely. Kept sheep all me life and they don't normally go over the wire like that, not unless they're spooked."

"And these weren't panicked?"

"Weren't no evidence to say that they had been. The rest were all right, and the fence wasn't damaged."

Brian looked across the muddy yard at a number of ewes that bleated and jostled each other in a small pen. "Is that where they went from?" he asked.

"No, they're just in for lambing. The ewes went from the field at the back of the house. Same field as the others were killed in."

"What do you think happened to them?"

Eric stared with a worried expression at the restless ewes. "I just don't know, and that's the truth of it."

* * *

The following day Brian was relating the conversation to Jill Forsythe over a drink in the *Fox and Hounds*.

"Could a big cat snatch a full grown ewe?" he asked.

She nodded. "Easily. A leopard can carry an antelope for a fair distance." She sipped her drink thoughtfully, sucking the liquid through the ice cubes against her closed teeth. "You know, there's something else, something that . . . . .." she paused, as if unwilling to put into words what she was thinking.

"What?"

"Hey, Brian, want a fill up?" Jim was propping up the bar, grinning across at him. "What are you drinking.... er..."

"Jill. Jill Forsythe," she introduced herself.

"What are you drinking, Jill?" He picked up her glass and sniffed. "Ah, a connoisseur. The peaty water of the lochs, no less."

"Diluted with the juice of the citrus," Jill said with a smile.

"Tch, tch. Sacrilege." With a grin Jim wandered back to the bar, ordered the drinks and then carried them across. "There you are, and when you get fed up with this bundle of laughs, I'll be waiting at the bar."

Brian raised his glass to his boss and then turned his attention back to Jill. "What was it you were about to say?"

Jill looked perplexed. "I don't know, it's completely slipped my mind, whatever it was."

"It couldn't have been important then."

She peered anxiously into her glass. "No. No, I suppose not." Yet deep inside her there was a worry, a half-buried niggle, that she couldn't quite reach.

* * *

It wasn't until late that night, when she was home and in bed, that the thought suddenly surfaced and she recalled clearly what she had been going to say.

She sat up in bed, fully awake and cold with shock. She tried to push the idea back into her subconscious, but it refused to bury itself again. She looked at the clock: it was three in the morning.

The witching hour.

The time that the body is at its lowest ebb.

The time of death.

It seemed a terrible thing to do, cruel, but she had no choice. She couldn't stand the thought alone till morning - she had to share it, be told it was wrong. She lifted the 'phone and dialled Brian's home number. From his slurred speech she knew she had woken him.

"Hello."

"Brian, it's Jill here. I'm sorry to call you at this time but I've got to talk to you." Brian was immediately wide awake.

"What's wrong? Something's happened?"

"There's nothing wrong, not actually, now anyway. But I've got to talk to you."

"Well, talk."

"No, not on the 'phone. Can you come round?"

He looked at the clock. "What, now?"

"Please. Right away. I'm sorry, but I need to see you." She sounded like a small, frightened child, and he felt an overwhelming protectiveness towards her. He was already pulling on his jeans.

"I'm on my way."

A quarter of an hour later he screeched to a halt outside her isolated cottage. The lights were on and the front door opened as he walked up the narrow path. She stood waiting for him, wrapped in a warm velvet dressing gown, her face devoid of make-up, her blonde hair tumbling loosely around her shoulders. It wasn't the sleek sophisticated vet he was seeing; it was the little Jill of years ago, who, having woken from a nightmare, wanted her parents to reassure her.

Without thinking, he threw his arms around her and crushed her to him, feeling her slender body trembling like a captive bird as she burrowed against his chest.

"It's all right, whatever it is," he murmured, brushing the perfumed softness of her hair with his lips. He led her inside and closed the door, shutting away the cold and the darkness of the night.

"I'm sorry." She looked up at him and smiled ruefully, brushing a wisp of hair from her eyes. "You must think I'm an awful baby." She pushed herself away from him reluctantly and led the way into the kitchen. "I've made some coffee." The dog gave a low growl and stood alert, watching the stranger in his kitchen, but making no attempt to attack. Brian paused in the doorway. He didn't mind dogs, never had been afraid of them, but this one was something different and rather unexpected. It was massive, the size of a Shetland pony with a huge head and bull neck, the muscles rippling under the gleaming fawn skin.

"Oh, don't mind Sam, he's gentle as a lamb. Once he knows you are a friend he'll settle." She clicked her fingers and at once the massive animal went to his mistress's side where he stood protectively, watching Brian from strange golden eyes.

"I know you said you had a great dane, but I didn't think it was going to be that size. He's the size of a bloody horse!"

She laughed, and he was relieved to see some of the strain lifted from her face. "Yes, he is a little large, even by great dane standards. That's how I got him. He outgrew his former home and his owners couldn't find anyone willing to take him on. They asked me to put him down." She patted the huge silky head and the dog turned adoring eyes towards her. "He was only two, and he's such a big softie. Well, I couldn't destroy him, and I couldn't find a home for him, so I adopted him." It was obviously a very successful arrangement. "Here, pat him, he won't bite."

Rather gingerly Brian reached out a hand and cautiously patted the dog which promptly wriggled with pleasure, pushing hard against his legs, nearly knocking him off balance.

"Hey! Steady boy. You will have me over." The dog twisted and whacked Brian with a powerful sideswipe from its rear.

"You'd better sit down before you're knocked down." Jill smiled as she put two cups of coffee on the table. Brian shoved the oversized hound aside and just made the chair before being lashed by the whip-like tail. "Sam! Enough. Settle." At his mistress's command, the dog threw himself down on the floor with a resounding crash, to lie with his head on his huge paws, watching them.

"It's a bloody good job you don't live in an upstairs flat." Brian laughed, then he looked serious. "Now, what is the problem that couldn't wait till morning?"

"I'm sorry. I couldn't cope with it alone and there wasn't anyone else I could talk to."

"I'm glad you called me," he said softly. "What's happened?"

She stared unhappily at her cup. "It was something you said, in the pub, just before your boss came over. Do you remember?"

"I remember Jim but I don't remember what I was saying."

"Well, I do. I was just about to remark on it when we were interrupted, and then I couldn't remember what I was going to say."

"And now you have?" She nodded miserably.

"And now I have."

"So?" he waited expectantly, but she seemed to have difficulty in forming the words.

"You remember you were talking about ewes disappearing, about them being snatched up suddenly and vanishing without trace. Well, that is almost exactly what a policeman said about the disappearance of Andrew Roberts." She pushed a crumpled newspaper cutting towards him. "You reported it yourself."

Brian read his own article:

```
'A police spokesman said, "It's as if the boy had been
spirited away, snatched into space! We've just nothing to
go on."'
```

He now realised why Jill had made that frightened call.

"The cat!" he breathed, and Jill knew he understood. They sat in silence for a while, the only sounds the ticking clock, the hum of the freezer and the occasional whimper from the sleeping dog. At last Jill spoke.

"What can we do?" she asked. Brian shook his head.

"I don't know. We've no real proof. Nothing tangible to go on. Only a suspicion and a gut feeling."

"But it's more than that. Everything fits."

Brian thought about the bike lying tumbled across the lane, almost as if the boy had been lifted from the saddle, leaving the bike to topple over on its side. Snatched into space? A huge cat leaping over the hedge, or dropping out of a tree, taking the boy completely by surprise. There would be no time for the boy to scream. The weight of the cat would probably snap his neck. It would all have been over in less than a second. The boy lifted up in the powerful jaws, carried as a domestic cat carries a mouse, across the lane in a leap, over the hedge and away. No sound, no tyre marks, nothing, just the bike left lying in the road. Snatched into space?

"God," he sighed.

"And no body," said Jill softly. "At least nothing the police would recognise as a body. Just a few splintered bones with nothing to suggest they were human," Suddenly the kitchen lost its warmth and cosiness, it became chill, a small pool of light hemmed in by the menacing blackness beyond the shelter of the four walls. They stared at one another across the scrubbed pine table and Brian reached out and gently squeezed her hand. She smiled gratefully.

"I'm sorry to be such a baby. It's just that I couldn't cope with thinking about it alone. I keep seeing that young boy laughing in the papers and on the posters the police circulated. He looks so young, so full of life, and then I keep thinking of him being torn to pieces, eaten ...... it is so horrible!"

"We could be wrong," murmured Brian.

"We're not though, are we?" She shuddered. "I know I'm being irrational. After all, it would have been an instantaneous death. He would never have known what attacked him, rather like a hit and run accident. But somehow the thought of it is awful, the idea of him being eaten."

"I know exactly what you mean, however illogical. If it were an animal, then it would have been better for the lad than being taken by a pervert. Death would have been quick. He wouldn't have been sexually assaulted, raped or tortured. It would have been a swift, clean, and in a way, a natural death."

"It still seems so much more horrible, the thought of his body being eaten." Jill's voice faltered emotionally. "It doesn't make sense. The boy would have suffered no more than someone being killed in a road traffic accident. I suppose it's because in our modern world we have grown to accept rape and murder as a normal part of our civilisation. Perverts are a part of our society, but we've still got hang-ups about the disposal of our dead. Bodies are more sacred dead than alive, if you know what I mean?"

Brian sighed. "I know exactly what you mean." Jill looked down at the table, refusing to meet his gaze.

"Look, will you ....." She paused, embarrassed. "For Christ's sake, I can't face being alone at the moment! Will you stay the night? Please."

It was difficult to know who made the first move. Somehow they seemed to meet in the middle, then she was sobbing in his arms, he was holding her, soothing her, like a father comforting a child in distress, crooning softly, rocking gently. Sam looked anxiously, but he watched his mistress relax in Brian's arms, the dog settled back down to sleep. He was content to let humans sort out their own problems.

That first night together they made love, not tenderly but urgently, as if that might shut away the world with its fears and horrors. As he thrust against her, she whimpered, clawing at his back, not fighting him but dragging him into her, trying to merge their bodies, to blend flesh with flesh, bone fusing with bone, mind with mind. At last, exhausted, they slept, wrapped in each other's arms, their skin slippery with sweat that beaded, glistening like dew on their backs and sprawled limbs. It hadn't been love, more purging of their bodies, a frantic escape from reality.

They awoke to find the warm sunlight streaming through the window, falling in pools of golden light on to the coverlet. Brian opened his eyes first, surprised for the moment to find himself in a strange bed and almost shocked to see Jill's head resting on his chest. He gently lifted away the tumbled strands of hair from her face and ran his finger across her cheek. She murmured slightly, twisting her body as she snuggled against him.

"Morning," She opened her blue eyes and tilted her head, gazed up at him. He nuzzled through her tangled hair to kiss her. "Breakfast, or ....." He pressed her breast in the cup of his hand.

"Or," she murmured, snuggling her body against his, her breast thrusting against his hand, her fingers running lightly along his body, across his hips to his thighs. This time they made love gently, slowly and with meaning, and when they had finished, there was no need for words between them. Something had happened, a relationship had been formed and cemented. He felt overwhelming desire to own her, to protect her. She, who had always been so independent, suddenly wanted to be owned, used and desired. The chemistry was complete.

After showering together, they sat in the warm kitchen, munching toast and drinking coffee, just looking at one another, bewildered by the force of their own emotions. It had happened so suddenly, so completely, they were like people in shock.

"I just wish it hadn't been something so horrible that brought us together," murmured Jill sadly. "Somehow it seems wrong, almost indecent, being so happy at a time like this."

"Like screwing in a churchyard on somebody's grave."

She raised an eyebrow. "I never have for comparison," she commented. "Have you?"

He grinned. "No. But I can imagine it." He linked fingers with hers. "The King is dead. Long live the King!"
"What?"

"Life must go on, I suppose. We shouldn't feel guilty about snatching what happiness we can from this whole bloody mess. We might need whatever strength we can get before long."

"Do you think things will get worse?" she asked.

He squeezed her hand. "I don't know what to think. If we are right, there's a man-eating big cat living wild around here. You know animals. Will it kill once and never kill again, or will it get a taste for human flesh?"

"I don't know. It is totally outside my experience. Some say cats turn man-eater once they have acquired the taste for human flesh. Others believe that big cats only kill humans for food when they are old and sick, unable to hunt their normal prey."

"If it has killed the Roberts boy, what now?" he persisted. She shook her head and shrugged helplessly.

"Maybe it will go back to sheep and never attack another human. There is no evidence to show it has attacked humans in the past. There seems to be no reason for it to start now."

They had no way of knowing that the answer was lost in a decaying ramshackle hut where Trapper's voice was stilled forever. The only voice that could have explained the change in the behaviour of the big cat.

"Before we panic, we need to be certain. Find out if the boy was attacked by a feral cat." Jill was desperate for the whole affair to become a nightmare from which they could both wake up.

"I suppose we could have a look around the area, see if we can find something the police might have missed," Brian said thoughtfully.

"What sort of thing?"

He shook his head. "I really don't know. Something, anything that might give us a clue."

"You mean a body?" asked Jill in a shocked whisper.

"No. Nothing as obvious as that. Hell, they might be a bit woolly headed at times but our police certainly couldn't have accidentally missed a body. They did a pretty thorough search, you know."

Jill suddenly hit the table with a bang, causing the cups to rattle in their saucers and the snoozing dog to look up, startled out of its dream of chasing rabbits. "They bloody well could, you know!" she exclaimed, staring at Brian with horrified eyes. "They certainly could have missed it!"

"Oh, come on Jill, be sensible. They went over the ground on hands and knees with a fine toothcomb. Even the police couldn't have missed a body. It would have been right under their noses." Jill stared at him.

"Oh no, it wouldn't," she said softly. "Not if we've a leopard loose. Quite the opposite in fact. It would have been right over their heads! Remember what I told you about big cats, they all have different eating habits. A leopard, as well as devouring its prey in a set pattern, nearly always dines high above the ground, taking its meal up into the branches of a tree."

Brian stared at her, "So you are telling me the boy's body could have been wedged up a tree while the police were searching the ground, with it stuck over their bloody heads?"

"It makes sense, after all, where is the last place anyone ever looks? Up."

Brian closed his eyes and sighed, "What are you planning to do today?"

Jill smiled with her mouth, though not with her eyes, "Going down to the woods," she suggested.

"I have a feeling that this will be no picnic," added Brain softly.

* * *

He was right. The combination of the wet spring and the police activities had churned the ground into a foot-deep morass of mud, littered with broken branches and torn up bushes. Only the trees themselves stood untouched in the wreckage of the wood; giants that towered over man's destruction of their environment. Glades that were once strewn with primroses now appeared like rutted scars, the earth chopped and slashed, the grass and plants torn and ripped from the soil, bluebell bulbs, like tiny onions, scattered around the surface, their newly sprouting green spears drying and withering in infancy.

"I'm glad I wore my wellies," gasped Jill as she heaved her feet out of the mud with squelching noises that sounded as if the earth had violent indigestion. She hauled herself from one tree trunk to another, trying unsuccessfully to find firmer ground. "This is hard going!"

"It must have been worse for the police, they had to crawl through it", Brian called back as he scrabbled over a fallen tree trunk and resting there, waited for her to catch up with him.

"Phew, I thought some of the farmyards I've been through were bad enough. They weren't even starters compared to this little lot."

Brian glanced around him, "It's too wet even for prints."

Where they had trodden, the ground was too soft to hold the shape of the soles of their boots for more than a few seconds before the impression filled with scummy red water, the sides collapsing, leaving only a dented surface. Jill panted up to the tree trunk and gratefully collapsed on to it.

"How on earth do we find anything in this jungle" she asked wearily as Brian brushed the wet earth from his trousers. "We know the police made a pretty good sweep of this area, but they weren't looking for anything a cat might have left behind."

"You mean like chewed bones or scratched trees?"

"Exactly, remember they were looking for places where a man could go, walking upright, not a cat on all fours". She shivered, and not just from the cold, as she wiped the mud from her face with an even muddier hand and looked around the desolate scene.

"You know, if we're right", she said thoughtfully, "the thing could be sitting over our heads right now".

It was a thought that Brian had been trying to avoid. "They only hunt at night, don't they?" he asked hopefully. Jill wasn't giving him any comfort.

"Do they?" she answered shortly. "I don't know what they do. The only live leopards I've ever seen have been safely behind bars, and they seem to be quite happy to dine in the daytime".

Suddenly Brian felt very puny and vulnerable. "You don't think it might ...?" his voice trailed off as he desperately peered up into the gloom above him.

"I don't know what to think," said Jill in a strained whisper, "I've never hunted big cats, I don't know anything about them, only what I've read and I've never read anything about big cat behaviour in the British countryside." Brian put a comforting arm around her and she snuggled against him.

"Do you want to go back?" he asked, but she shook her head.

"No, we've got to try and find out, and if we're right, get proof. It won't bring young Andrew back, but it might save the life of another youngster," she said with emotion.

"I love you," Brian murmured and kissed her muddy cheek. "Let's go on. We'll give it another two hours, then, no matter what, we call it off".

"How long have we been out?" Jill asked with a sniff.

Brian looked at his watch. "Nearly three hours, another couple of hours and it will be dusk. I don't think it a good idea to be around here then".

"Three hours?" echoed Jill miserably. "It feels much longer than that". She slid of the trunk, back into the deep mud, and wearily started plodding onwards with a deep sigh.

Within half-an-hour they reached higher ground and the going became firmer. For the first time they began to see tracks, evidence of the movement of numerous wild creatures - the tiny v-shaped slots of deer, slender dog shaped prints of foxes and the long clawed impressions left by the heavy waddling badger in its snuffling search for food. On a ridge overlooking the forestry land, they followed a winding narrow well-trodden path.

"Look at this," Brian crouched down and studied the ground carefully.

"What is it?" Jill peered over his shoulder.

"This print, it's like the one I found near the place where Amy Meakin came off her horse. See?" He brushed away some of the surrounding debris of leaves, revealing a large print about four inches across. "What made that?"

Jill bent down and examined the print before looking up and staring at him. "It's like a cat print," she said softly. "A huge cat print. See how the toe pads make a semi-circle around the half moon-shaped heel pad? That is like a cat's. A dog's toe pads are more to the front with a deep depression between them and the heel pad. Like those of foxes".

"So it is a cat".

"It is like a cat, but it does show the claws. Cats usually retract their claws when walking, which is how they keep them razor sharp. As far as I know, the only cat unable to retract its claws is the cheetah".

"So could we have a wild cheetah?"

"Not if the witnesses are to be believed," she replied slowly. "Cheetahs aren't black or dark coloured, they are golden brown with very noticeable spots. Whatever has been seen around here, it certainly wasn't a cheetah".

"So where does that leave us?"

She shook her head. "I just don't know," she said quietly. "I really don't know".

Brian straightened up. "Right, let's go a bit further and see if we can find anymore".

They found more than they bargained for. About a quarter of a mile along the path, they came to a clear stretch of firm mud across which had walked a large animal, leaving the perfect marks of its passage. The cat-like prints were sharp and clean, but it was not the large prints that made them catch their breaths in shock. Two sets of tiny prints, not much bigger than those of a domestic cat, followed the large ones, the small creatures appearing to trail so closely behind the bigger one, that at times the small were superimposed on the large. Jill looked at Brian in horror.

"Whatever it is, it's got young!" she said in a strangled whisper. Together they stood in the silence of the darkening forest, staring down at the tracks before them. Brian was the first to notice the failing light. He looked at his watch.

"Hell!" he explained. "We've got to get out of here". Jill wasn't going to argue. It was dusk, and whatever the creature was, dusk would be its most likely time for hunting. Already they might have left it too late.

"What's the quickest way back?" she asked, totally disorientated by the surrounding trees.

"It will take us too long to go back the way we've come," replied Brian anxiously. "If you don't mind the rough ground, I think we could reach the road quicker by cutting across this valley and going straight through the woods".

"Let's go then".

Already Jill was slithering down the bank through the tangled undergrowth, ignoring the grasping thorny fingers of the naked briars. It was hard going and they were both panting, their sides heaving painfully before long. Jill clasped her ribs, trying to ignore the cramp in her side. Without saying anything, they were conscious of the deepening gloom around them as the trees seemed to move closer together, growing thicker and impeding their progress, as if nature herself was against them. With his longer, stronger legs, Brian moved ahead, breaking the way for Jill. Finally, he grabbed her arm and pulled her along as she struggled after him. It was frightening how quickly the light seemed to be fading. Soon they were in a half-light, the shadows becoming solid velvety patches, objects disappearing in the dusk, to be replaced by an indistinct world of grey and black.

The big cat lay curled comfortably in the fork of a tree when she became aware of the sound of large bodies crashing past below her. She curled her lip in a silent snarl and wrinkled her nose, scenting the intruders as she peered down into the gloom, her ears pricked, her eyes bright and alert.

It was time to hunt and prey was close.

With a swift check on her sleeping cubs, lying tangled in a tight ball in the hollow at the heart of the tree, she leapt to the ground with effortless grace, despite her twisted rear leg. Pausing for a second to sniff the air, she sprang in the direction of the noise of the prey's passage through the undergrowth, running with a jerky movement, her injured leg stiffly drawn up. Her weight was carried on her three good legs, but she made good speed.

After her injury, the cat found movement difficult at first, but within a week or so, she had adjusted to her disability. Although she had lost a degree of mobility, especially on turning when chasing prey, she found she coped well enough. She had to choose her prey more carefully, however, and had no chance now when pitted against the fleet-footed deer or a weaving hare across open ground. Even the sheep on the hillside were fast for her, although nearer the house, where they were penned in by fencing that trapped them, she had no problem, especially with the young lambs that she could snatch away before their mothers even got wind of her presence.

She had also experimented with another sort of prey, soft skinned, without teeth or claws to defend itself. It was just such an easy prey that she could scent on the wind ahead of her.

It was Jill who first detected the sound of movement in the forest. She paused, gasping as she leant against a fallen tree. She held her breath and listened. Behind her there was the cracking of branches and the sound of panting. Ahead of her, Brian waved.

"Come on" he yelled. "There's a hedge here and someone's garden, so we must have reached the road".

"Brian, I can hear something. It's following us!" she screamed.

He turned and crashed back towards her. "Just your imagination," he shouted. "Come on we've nearly made it".

"No, listen, listen," she sobbed, almost hysterical. "There's something following us".

He caught hold of her arm. "Nonsense," he began, and then froze. Just behind them he heard a rustling of bushes and a soft throaty growl. "Oh my God!" he gasped. Grabbing Jill by the shoulders, he shook her, trying to get her to move. "Run. Run like hell! We can make that house. Do you hear me? Run!"

She stared at him numbly, her eyes glazed with terror, her limbs paralysed with fright and she shook her head.

"I can't, I can't!" she sobbed, tears furrowing the mud on her cheeks. With a sudden fury, he slapped her face.

"Run, you stupid cow! Run!"

The effect of the blow was like an electric shock. With a cry, she stumbled forward and blindly began to run, Brian pushing and shoving her ahead of him.

They reached the hedge and plunged bodily into it, smashing their way through the thorny twigs, regardless of the whiplash of the branches and the tearing of their clothes and skin.

Ahead was a stretch of lawn which they raced across. A large, isolated house loomed out of the gloom. Brian pulled Jill with him by superhuman effort. He could hear the animal pounding after them. Jill was doubled up, gasping, but he wouldn't let her pause. Almost wrenching her arm from its socket, he dragged her towards the house. Screaming for help, they reached the front door and hammered on it. The sound of the knocker echoed with hollow thuds.

There was no answer.

"There's no one there," sobbed Jill as she collapsed in the porch. Brian leant on the bell but it made no sound. "It's no use. There's no one to help us".

Behind them the big cat skidded to a halt. She knew the grounds of the house well, for this was home territory. She crouched low, her tail lashing the ground, choosing her prey. She knew that both of the tender-skinned sweet-tasting animals were trapped against the wall. She growled low in the chest, a deep warning growl to let any other perspective diners in the area know that this was her meal and hers alone. Keep away.

Jill sank to her knees, whimpering, watching the dark shape of the animal as it belly crawled towards them. Brian swore under his breath and then hurled himself at the glass pane in the top half of the door. As his shoulder hit it, the glass showered all around them. Oblivious of the broken splinters, he thrust his hand through and reached for the lock.

"Come on. Quick!" he shouted as the door swung open. He grabbed Jill and threw her into the darkened hallway were she crashed across the floor, knocking over unseen furniture. He leapt in after her, slamming the broken door behind him just as the cat made her spring. With a furious scream, the beast struck the door, her claws ripping the wood of the lower panels. She drew back, bewildered, unable to work out how her prey had vanished. She sniffed, tracing the scent to beyond the door.

She directed her frustration against the heavy panels, tearing and gouging at the wood, biting at the frame with her dagger like fangs.

"Oh, dear God, it's coming in," sobbed Jill as she crouched in the hall, watching the door shake and rattle with the force of the beast hurling against it. With a report like a pistol firing, a crack appeared in the wooden panel and a black paw hooked through the broken glass, the claws scraping against the sharp splinters. Slithers of shattered glass fell to the floor as the paw scrabbled to get a grip. There was a screech as part of the head appeared, the lips drawn back in a snarl revealing pink jaws laced with huge curved teeth.

"For Christ's sake, let's get out of here!"

Brian pulled Jill away from the door, breaking the almost hypnotic effect the sight of the cat was having on her. He grabbed at a light switch, but nothing happened; the electricity was cut off.

"Come on. Our best chance is upstairs," He half pushed and half hauled her up the carpeted stairs.

"What's the use? It's coming in," she wailed. "It's going to kill us!"

"It's not supernatural," he yelled back, trying to be heard above the cat's furious screams. "It's only a bloody cat. We can beat it!"

"How?" she moaned. "How?" He didn't answer. He paused on the landing, trying to get his bearings in the darkness of the corridor, then grabbing her, he dragged her towards an open door, flinging her inside and slamming it shut just as he heard the sound of smashing wood when the front door finally gave way to the onslaught of the exasperated cat.

Suddenly everything became quiet; all he could hear was Jill sobbing in the far corner. As his eyes adjusted to the gloom, he could see her crouched, curled in a tight ball against the wall in a foetal position. He looked around at the contents of the room - it was a bedroom full of heavy old-fashioned furniture. As well as turning the key that was in the lock, he also dragged an old chest of drawers across the door. Then he listened. He presumed the cat was prowling around downstairs, trying to locate them. It would only be a matter of time before the beast tried the stairs; after all, what was a flight of stairs to a creature that could carry a full-size buck thirty feet up a tree?

Downstairs the cat was investigating the place room by room. Everything smelt of the soft-skinned prey, but combined with other strange smells, which she didn't recognise. She leapt up on the polished table, her feet slipping and skidding from under her, and tipped the entire thing over as she sprang off, sending the dining chairs scattering in all directions. She snapped at one, as if it were attacking her, and spat out a mouthful of splinters. The noise of the furniture being dragged about overhead attracted her attention and she padded silently over the carpet, along the hall to the foot of the stairs.

She could smell her prey strongly now, the bitter sweet smell of human sweat and fear. She sniffed at the steps cautiously, a low warning rumble in her throat, before venturing upwards, following the scent.

Brian heard the growl as he pulled the old-fashioned heavy bedstead across the room to reinforce the pile of furniture against the door, then he took the coverlet and pillows over to where Jill was still curled in a frightened ball.

"It's all right, sweetheart. It can't get us now," he whispered, taking her in his arms.

"I'm sorry to be so useless," she sobbed. "I didn't think I could ever be so frightened of an animal." He ran his fingers through her hair and tilted her tear-stained face up to him, kissing her gently.

"It's all right. I'm frightened too".

"But I'm just useless, useless! If it hadn't been for you I would have just waited for it to kill me. Just waited to die," she sobbed, trembling uncontrollably, "I'm so ashamed".

He held her to him, crushing her against his chest. "Sweetheart, you mustn't be. Christ, I was so scared I nearly shit myself".

She looked at him in horror. "You didn't?"

He laughed, feeling her relax a little in his arms. "No. But it was a near thing. Any more days like this and I'm into pampers!"

Outside the door came a muffled growl and a scratching sound.

"It's still out there!" she screamed, clinging to him.

The cat paced outside the door, lashing out in annoyance at wall and woodwork, tearing great strips from the wallpaper. She was frustrated, able to scent her prey but unable to reach it. She sat down and tilted her head with a snarl, laying back her ears. At once a terrible screech filled the air, the sound rolling and echoing from room to room in the empty house. Brian and Jill cowered together, watching the door in horrible fascination, waiting for the razor sharp claws to rip through the panels.

Nothing further happened. Cuddled together, clinging to one another, wrapped in the feather quilt, they finally fell into an uneasy sleep. Across the woods, the moon hung suspended in the velvet darkness of the star-spangled sky, her silvery light frosting the treetops. A ewe called nervously for her lamb, listening for the bleating of her lost baby. The lamb was beyond its mother's help. The big cat limped across the wooded valley, the dead lamb dangling from her jaws. Already she had forgotten her frustrated anger at missing her first prey and she was eager to return to her growing cubs.

Brian and Jill awoke stiff and cold, still curled together, to find the daylight pouring through the uncurtained window, shafts of gold falling on to the worn carpet, dust particles dancing in the beams. They both remembered the horror of the night's events the moment they opened their eyes and were conscious of their surroundings.

"Do you think it's still there?" whispered Jill hoarsely. Brian shook his head.

"Not a chance. It will have long gone. We're quite safe now". Despite his assurances, he was in no hurry to remove the furniture blocking the door. He stood up, stretched and then listened intently. The only sound was the birdsong from the garden. Relieved, he helped Jill to her feet. They both felt sore, their bodies bruised and aching.

"I wonder whose house we are in," Jill whispered, looking around in the sunlight and seeing the room clearly for the first time. It was a very old-fashioned bedroom with heavy Edwardian furniture, a fact that they were aware had probably saved their lives. It didn't bear thinking about how they might fared if the house owner had favoured the flimsy plywood units and built in wardrobes of modern day.

"Obviously someone elderly," said Brian as he glanced at the collection of framed photographs littering the dressing table and the mantelpiece.

Jill gave a horrified gasp. "You don't think they are here and it got them, do you?"

"I shouldn't think so. They would have come out to see what all the noise was about when we broke in".

"But suppose they are deaf," Jill suggested anxiously. "Some old people can't hear anything without their hearing aids and they wouldn't have been wearing them in bed. Or they could have taken sleeping tablets".

Brian frowned. "No. There isn't any electricity, so the house must have been shut up for some time".

Cautiously he dragged the heavy furniture away from the door, wondering at the speed with which he had manoeuvred it into place in his panic. It took all his courage to remove the barricade, while listening nervously, waiting for the slightest creak that would give warning of an attack. But all was quiet.

"My God, look at that!" exclaimed Jill in a shocked voice. Brian said nothing, he just stared. The door was splintered, chunks had been torn or bitten from the framework and the panels were raked and gouged. It didn't take much to picture what would have happened to them if the cat had affected an entry. They walked slowly along the passageway, noting the torn and shredded wallpaper and the ripped carpet. The animal had certainly taken its fury out the house when it was frustrated in its efforts to reach them. Silently they checked through the house, room by room, terrified of finding evidence of occupancy, but it appeared the owner was safely away. In fact, the only sign of recent life was the still connected telephone.

"I'll see if I can find the main electric switch," said Brian, "then we can brew up. You give the police a ring and ask them to get out here". He looked around at the smashed dining table and broken chairs littering the room. "I think we've got enough proof to show them when they come, even if we haven't got a body to present them with".

"Don't, Brian. Don't! I keep thinking of that poor boy".

Purely by chance it was Mrs Agnes Briant's old friend P.C. George Wells who answered the 'phone at the station that morning. He hadn't given a thought to missing old Mrs Briant's daily reports, not with the missing child enquiry keeping everyone on their toes and on overtime. It was only when he glanced at the clock, and saw it was nearly nine, that he remembered Agnes Briant and her calls. Even so, it was with a feeling of some surprise that he heard a young woman's voice instead of that of a faded, tired old lady.

"Please, can you send someone over. We've been attacked by a leopard".

P.C. Wells froze, his lips tightening with anger. So someone had a sense of humour, did they? "Are you making a complaint about being attacked, madam?" he asked coldly.

"Of course I am," said the woman's voice, verging on a high-pitched note of hysteria. "It tried to kill us, so what do you think I'm doing?"

"Perhaps playing silly games," suggested P.C. Wells calmly.

"Oh yes, I make a point of trying to get eaten every day," said Jill bitterly. "Will you please send someone round?"

"We are rather busy at the moment," answered Wells, trying to keep his temper. "May I suggest you play games with your friends and not waste police time?"

"Look, I don't care whether or not you think I'm a nutter, will you please send someone round here so they can see for themselves?" Jill almost screamed. At that moment Brian walked in.

"Electricity's on. Fancy a cuppa?" he asked.

"Will you speak to this pompous twit on the end of this line?" Jill exploded, not caring that the policeman was able to hear every word. "The stupid man thinks I'm having him on!"

"You go and find a kettle, I'll talk to him". Brian took the 'phone from her. "The kitchen's through there".

"I would like to point out to the lady, sir, that there are penalties for wasting police time".

"Who am I speaking to?"

"Police Constable Wells".

"Well, P.C. Wells" said Brian sarcastically, "I should like to point to you that we are well aware of the penalties. Now will you please send someone round here immediately. As a citizen of this country, I have a statutory right to ask the police for protection, and that is what I am doing".

George Wells sighed. "Very well, sir. Can you give me the address?"

"Ah..." Brian paused. "I can give you the telephone number but I don't know the address".

The policeman's voice took on a strained quality. "Are you saying you have been attacked by a wild beast, your lives are in danger and you are demanding police protection, but you don't know your address?"

"That about sums it up," said Brian cheerfully. "Look, we were out walking in Whiteoaks wood yesterday when we were chased by a large black animal like a panther. We broke into a house for shelter. I don't know the address, the place is empty, but the cat got in after us and has torn the place to shreds. If you send someone here, they'll see the damage for themselves and then they can decide what did it".

"You are saying you broke into an empty house, sir?" the policeman asked quietly. "Are you confessing to a felony?"

"I'll confess to bloody murder if it'll make you send someone over here!"

"But, over where?"

"God! Can't you look it up from the telephone number?"

"What is the number?" George Wells sighed, heartily wishing it was his day off. Brian read the number on the telephone in front of him. The policeman drew a sudden sharp intake of breath. It was a number he recognised all too well. "Is that where you are now?"

"Oh no," Brian replied sarcastically. "I'm reading the number through binoculars from half a mile away".

"What does the house look like? The contents, I mean?"

Brian looked around. "Before or after the rampaging cat?" he asked.

"I mean is it a small house, a large house, modern or old-fashioned? What sort of furniture?"

"Oh, old-fashioned, a big rambling place full of huge heavy old furniture," said Brian.

George Wells whistled. "Sounds as if you are in old Mrs Briant's place. Did you say you were attacked by a black panther?"

"That's what we've been trying to get through to you, yes. I honestly don't know if it was a panther or not, but it was certainly black, the size of an Alsatian dog, a cat, and very nasty in temperament".

"And you say it attacked you at Mrs Briant's place?"

"If this is Mrs Briant's place, yes. And attacking is putting it mildly. The bloody thing attempted to eat us".

P.C. Wells interrupted him. "No one has put you up to this?"

"What the hell for?" exploded Brian. "Look, we're ringing to say we've broken into an empty house to avoid providing a bloody big cat with its dinner. The place has been wrecked by the fucking animal, we're not going out of this place without a car, just in case it's still hanging around, and if you've any sense, you will send someone with a gun."

George Wells made a quick decision. "Very well, I'll come myself. Just stay put."

"And you're bringing a weapon?"

"One thing at a time," said the policeman resignedly. "I first want to see the damage you claim the beast has caused." He put the 'phone down with a bang.

Brian and Jill were sipping their third cup of Mrs Briant's tea when they heard the car drive up the gravel entrance to the house.

"Thank God we've got some action," sighed Jill. "I couldn't face another night here and nothing is going to get me walking back those woods."

Brian leant across and kissed her cheek. "I think I might prefer the walk to another cup of milkless tea." He grinned at her.

P.C. George Wells stood in the doorway, gazing aghast at the smashed and splintered front door. "Good grief!" he said, "did you do that to get in?" Brian gestured to the damage.

"I only had to smash the glass panel to get the door open, the beast did the rest trying to get at us."

The policeman wandered from room to room as if in a state of shock. They showed him what was left of the bedroom door behind which they'd barricaded themselves.

"If I hadn't seen it for myself," he said quietly. "I wouldn't have believed it. Poor old Mrs Briant."

"She has lost a lot of stuff and her house has been ripped about a bit, but at least she wasn't here at the time. It could have been worse you know. If she'd been here, it would have certainly have killed her," said Jill in a hushed voice.

"Oh, it's not that exactly. I was thinking about the poor old lady," explained P.C.Wells, scratching his chin. "You see, for months she has regularly reported seeing a black panther."

"So why didn't someone do something about the bloody thing?"

"We didn't believe her," replied the policeman regretfully.

"Well it's obviously been living around here for quite a while," retorted Brian angrily.

"Looks like it. I should have listened instead of letting them put her away".

"Put her away?" echoed Jill.

The constable shuffled his feet uneasily. "No one believed Mrs Briant, including me," he said ruefully. "We all thought she was just a bit dotty. In the end the social worker decided the old lady should be in hospital rather than alone in this big house, so they shipped her off".

Jill looked horrified. "Just because she claimed to have seen the cat?"

"Fraid so. Mind, the poor old biddy was a bit isolated out here, so she'll probably be better off in care, but of course she won't see it that way. She loved her home, did Agnes Briant." He looked around at the mess, the smashed furniture and ripped carpets, and sighed. "God knows how they'll get this lot cleaned up for her to come home."

"They'll let her come home then?" asked Jill, thinking what a shock it would be for the old lady to see what had happened to so many of her cherished possessions.

"Should do, for her age she's in pretty good nick, but they thought her mind was gone".

"Because of the cat?" asked Brian.

George Wells nodded. "Because of the cat," he agreed. "That's why they put her in a mental hospital rather than an old folk's home. Because she kept claiming to see a big cat".

"Poor thing," sighed Jill. "It must have been dreadful for her to know she was seeing something and yet have everyone believe she was round the bend."

"I think that should be our first port of call," said Brian, "to go and see the old lady and her doctors."

"I'll go with you," offered P.C. Wells. "First I'll have to get someone round to sort this lot out and secure the place."

"It's not going to be easy," remarked Brian as he looked thoughtfully out the window towards the woods.

"That is an understatement," the policeman muttered gloomily. "Where on earth do we start?"

It was a problem his superiors were to face in a similar way.

* * *

The hospital was a grim and forbidding building, a throwback from the old workhouse days. The grey granite, prison-like walls were surrounded by acres of lawns, dotted with scattered flowerbeds.

They drove up the winding road towards the main building, passing numerous shuffling figures walking in small groups or isolated lonely individuals. Few even glanced at the police car as it passed, though one or two pairs of eyes looked up, revealing a terrible, sad, blank expression. Like lost souls, Jill thought with a shiver. The patients weren't all elderly, but all had had the same shuffling gait and gave off a feeling of hopelessness and lack of purpose.

"How awful," whispered Jill, clutching Brian's hand. "They all look the same."

"Not when you get to know them," said George cheerfully. "My wife used to be a mental nurse and she loved her patients. She said they all had terrific personalities once you got to know them. I suppose it is like anyone. You have to see below the surface."

"Like the old saying, beauty is only skin deep," muttered Brian. "I know you are right, but just seeing them, seeing the surface. I understand what Jill means. Somehow they are frightening. It's like seeing robots rather than people."

The police car swung into the gravel parking space outside the stone carved main entrance and they got out. Both Jill and Brian were suddenly very conscious of their mud-streaked torn clothing and dirty faces.

"I wish I had gone home and got changed," said Jill, feeling embarrassed as the bleached and starched nurse rustled over to meet them.

"Good morning, officer. Can I help you?" Her eyes passed disapprovingly over Jill and Brian, and with amusement they realised that she thought the police had escorted them to be admitted.

P.C. Wells cleared his throat. "You have an elderly patient, a Mrs Agnes Briant. I'd like to speak urgently to the doctor concerned with her case."

"I see." The plump nurse looked curiously at the three of them. "Do you know which ward Mrs Briant is in?"

The policeman shook his head. "I'm sorry, no."

The nurse gave a deep sigh. "Will you take a seat. I'll try and find who the doctor is and if he's available. How do you spell the patients name?"

It seemed a long wait, much longer than the old walnut framed wall clock suggested. They pooled resources and collected enough change to buy three cups of coffee from the vending machine, coffee that - to Brian's surprise - tasted like reasonable instant. He began to wonder about the machine in his office. Was it accidental that the hospital coffee was better, or did Jim do something diabolical to the staff supplies to put them off the idea of coffee breaks? His suspicions were interrupted when the nurse re-appeared in half an hour.

"Dr Ellis will be down in a minute to have a word with you. He's senior consultant psychiatrist involved with Mrs Briant."

Dr Ellis took fifteen minutes, rather than one, to appear.

"Good afternoon, officer. Sorry to have kept you waiting so long, I'm afraid I had a slight emergency on my hands. I understand you wish to speak to me about Mrs Briant."

George Wells nodded. "Could we go somewhere a little more private?"

"Of course. Of course. Just through here to my office." Dr Ellis beamed. He was a bland, plump, elderly man, his face almost devoid of any expression other than gentle tolerance and understanding. It is as if over the passage of years his professional mask had become a permanent fixture over his real face, hiding forever any real emotion he might be feeling. His office was a perfect match for him, neat and tidy, files stacked on dust free shelves, the desk Formica topped, modern and totally out of character with the Victorian half panelled room. He seated himself in a comfortable swivel chair behind his desk and gestured to the others to pull up assorted chairs.

"Now," he beamed. "Just how can I assist you?"

George Wells glanced at the other two before speaking. "Well, I think it's rather more like us helping you. You, I understand are responsible for Mrs Briant's medical welfare."

Dr Ellis nodded. "Yes, I admitted her. Sweet old lady. No trouble, no trouble at all. Just a little unwell, that's all. Often happens as people get older. Quite normal to be a little abnormal, as you might say."

He grinned happily at his own joke and his listeners got the impression it was a well tried one, that he was an actor launched on a familiar dialogue.

"I believe you admitted her because she thought she kept seeing very large cats in her garden," the constable went on.

"You obviously know her history. Apart from the problem of cats, she seems to behave a perfectly normal manner."

"She is normal," interrupted Jill bitterly. "Perfectly normal."

Dr Ellis interlocked his fingers and rested both hands lightly on the desk in front of him. "Apart from her obsession, I completely agree with you"

"It isn't an obsession," said Jill. "She is not imagining a big cat, she has seen it."

Dr Ellis raised his eyebrows. He took in Jill's rather dishevelled appearance and, wondering if the police had delivered another patient to him, said simply: "Indeed?"

George Wells leant forward. "The fact is, Dr Ellis, there appears to be evidence that a large panther-like cat is in fact living wild in the woods near Mrs Briant's home."

"There's no appears about it," commented Brian quietly. "We've seen it, been attacked by it."

Dr Ellis's face did not alter. Keeping the bland expression, only his eyes betrayed the bewilderment as he looked at the policeman, who nodded in agreement.

"I haven't seen the beast myself but I have seen the damage caused to Mrs Briant's house. The place was torn apart."

"By a big black cat?" asked Dr Ellis calmly.

"A black panther," stated Jill firmly. "It attacked and chased us and damn nearly killed us!"

"In Mrs Briant's house?"

Brian looked the doctor straight in the eye. "It smashed open the door to try and get at us."

Dr Ellis rubbed his nose thoughtfully. "You are both relatives of Mrs Briant?" he asked.

"No, neither of us have ever met the lady," Jill replied.

"Then forgive me, but why were you at her house?" the doctor asked, leaning back in his chair in an over-relaxed manner.

"We didn't know we were at the time," explained Brian. "We were in the woods when this panther started after us, so we made for the nearest house. In fact, it's the only house in the area. Everything was locked up but with a killer cat at our heels, we broke in and took shelter in a bedroom. The cat went in after us, and when it couldn't get at us, it tore the place to bits."

"We only found out it was Mrs Briant's place when we rang the police this morning," said Jill quietly. Even in the security of the hospital office, she didn't like remembering the horror of the night before.

"I took the call," P.C. Wells said firmly. "First off, I thought someone was having me on, especially when they told me they were 'phoning from Mrs Briant's house. However, when I got there and saw the damage..." he sighed. "Well, I can't truthfully think of anything else but a large clawed and fierce animal that could be responsible."

"Vandals?" suggested the doctor mildly. George Wells shook his head.

"No chance. It's clawed great chunks out of the woodwork, actually ripped the wood."

Jill leant forward. "So you see, poor Mrs Briant wasn't off her head. She really was seeing the cat. It's just no one would believe her."

Dr Ellis looked thoughtfully at his desk. "I see. Your point is that if the big black cat is living wild near Mrs Briant's house, then that is what she saw. If she really saw it, then there's nothing wrong with her?"

"Exactly!" exclaimed Jill. "In fact the old lady has no obsessions at all."

The doctor sighed. "It is a pity all this didn't come out before she came here. The trouble is she isn't a voluntary patient. As you know, she has been admitted under the Mental Health Act, so I can't just authorise you to take her home. Things will have to go through the normal channels." He paused. "There's another point to be considered too, Mrs Briant might have been in her right mind when reporting the cat, but not being believed will have caused her mental stress. She could have genuine problems now."

"You mean, because no one would believe her when she was telling the truth, then she might really have flipped now?" asked Brian, horrified.

"It's possible," Dr Ellis said softly." He stood up like a teacher dismissing his class. "Well now, I think the best thing is if we go and have a chat with the patient. If you'd like to follow me..." He led the way out of the room.

They walked along pale green corridors where the gloss paint was peeling and flaking from the walls, past numerous fire doors leading towards the wards. Identical shuffling figures to those in the grounds seemed to be wandering aimlessly from place to place. Although a few were clad in dressing gowns, most were draped in ill-fitting suits, or wrapped in shapeless dresses. The doctor led the group through the double glass doors into a large brightly-lit room which was crammed full of assorted metal framed chairs and numerous wheelchairs. The place wasn't exactly a hive of activity, although the room was full. Most of the patients, mainly elderly women, were sitting staring into space, some rocking gently backwards and forwards. Some were knitting or sewing, their faces screwed into concentration at their tasks. A few were reading, some had books or newspapers but a number were intently studying children's books or comics.

"This is where our elderly and less active patients spend their day," explained Dr Ellis. "Our younger and brighter patients are in the workshops. We have quite a factory going, you know."

"Good afternoon doctor." A sister bustled up, obviously surprised at Dr Ellis's unscheduled appearance.

"Good afternoon, sister. Everything going smoothly?" She nodded, looking curiously at the three visitors.

"No problems. Mr Edwards has had to be sent back to the ward. He is a little poorly this morning and I think it would be well to increase Mrs Will's sedation. She's shouting out loudly again, upsetting the others."

Dr Ellis nodded a trifle impatiently. "Fine. Fine, Sister. I'll make out a stronger prescription for her. Now we'd like to see Mrs Briant from ward two."

"Certainly Doctor. I believe she is in the other day room. Are you relatives?" she asked Jill.

"No, we just want to have a little chat with her, that's all."

Sister looked worriedly at the policeman. "I do hope there is nothing wrong with her family. She's such a lovely old lady and she dotes on her children."

George Wells smiled reassuringly. "No, there's nothing wrong. In fact, quite the opposite. These people might have some very good news for her."

"That's fine," the sister said, returning his smile. "Well I must get on. If you need me, doctor, I'll be in Ward One."

"Thank you, sister. I don't think we'll need to trouble you." He led the way through the double swing doors into a large airy room where the sun shining through the large Victorian bay windows formed pools of gold on the dull green floor tiles.

"I'm afraid we can't use carpet," apologised Dr Ellis. "Too many accidents. It makes it a little bleak but at least the staff can keep the place clean." He led them across the room, acknowledging the waves and nods of the seated patients.

"Have you come to take me away?" quavered a tiny bird-like old lady with her wispy grey hair tied up with bright pink ribbons.

"No Emily, you're quite safe today," the doctor shouted, patting the claw of a hand as it reached out to clutch his white coat. The old lady's eyes darted back and forth.

"They are coming, you know. I think it's today."

"I'll watch out for them and bring them in if they arrive," said Dr Ellis. "But you needn't go with them if you don't want to."

"I want to stay here," croaked Emily, tears flooding suddenly down her shrivelled cheeks. "They only wants me money. I want to stay with my friends."

"Then so you shall," soothed Dr Ellis, patting her hunched back before moving on.

"Stupid bloody bitch!" snapped a heavily built woman of about sixty - who was sitting in the next chair busily knitting. "You just encourage her, you do! She knows damn well there ain't no one coming for her, never has been and there never will be. Stupid old bat!"

"Now, now, Rosie," said Dr Ellis.

They moved on across the room to where Mrs Briant was sitting dozing by the window, a multi-coloured knitted blanket wrapped snugly around her legs. Dr Ellis touched her arm.

"Agnes, I've brought some visitors to see you."

Mrs Briant opened her eyes. "I wasn't asleep, doctor. I was just thinking, that's all. Remembering." She gazed up at the others and smiled when she saw Jill. "You're very beautiful, my dear," she said softly. "Isn't she beautiful, Doctor?"

Dr Ellis laughed at Jill's look of embarrassment. "Yes, she is."

Brian grinned. "I'll second that." Jill gave him a nudge.

"Shut up," she hissed.

"A policeman," murmured Mrs Briant. "I do believe it's the nice young man who came to see me at home. It is you, isn't it?" she asked. "My eyes aren't as good as they used to be and people in uniform all seem to look the same, don't they?"

"It's me all right, Mrs Briant," said George Wells cheerfully. "And I've brought this couple to have a little chat with you."

"How nice". Agnes patted some empty seats beside her. "Do sit down, my dears. I do so like talking to people."

"Ah, but these aren't just ordinary people," explained George. "They've got something very important to tell you."

"Really? What about?" she touched Jill's face gently. "Such a pretty young girl". She looked at Brian. "Are you married, you two?" she asked with the directness and the lack of tact of the elderly.

Brian laughed. "Not yet," he said with a wink. "But I'm working on the idea." Jill opened her mouth to comment and then changed her mind.

"You should get married as soon as possible," assured Mrs Briant seriously. "Life is so short, you know, you mustn't waste any of it." She sighed and settled back. Jill patted her mottled gnarled hand.

"We won't waste it, I promise," she said softly, avoiding Brian's eyes.

The old lady seemed satisfied. "Now, what did you young people want to talk to me about?"

"The cat," said Brian gently. "The cat you reported seeing in your garden."

"Ah, you mean the big black one." She smiled. "You know, they don't believe me, not even this nice policeman, or Dr Ellis here, no one believes me, but I did see it, plain as I am seeing you all." She gave another sad sigh. "I used to be frightened that it would hurt someone, attack a child maybe, but it didn't seem to be dangerous. It just seemed to want to live its own life and leave us to get on with ours. I suppose if it had attacked someone, they would have believed me then. It was because no one else saw it that they put me in here." She leant forward confidingly. "They tell me it's for my own good. I'm in a home because I'm too old to look after myself. But that isn't true. This isn't a home, it's a mental hospital, and they've put me in here because they think I'm mad." She smiled at Dr Ellis. "Never told you before that I knew, have I doctor? I just let you ask all your questions and fill in all your forms, but I've always known, since the first day."

Dr Ellis let his professional plastic face crack for a moment. "But if you've always known, Agnes, why didn't you say something? Tell us?"

Agnes Briant shrugged indifferently. "What would have been the point? It wouldn't have got me out of here, would it? As long as I told you the truth, told you about the cat, you would think I'm mad and as I've no intention of lying, not when I've got as near to my maker as I am now. Well….." she paused, "I don't suppose it makes much difference where I die."

"But if you'd said anything…" Dr Ellis let his voice trail away. The old lady was right. It wouldn't have made any difference to her situation. As long as the cat was considered to be a figment of her imagination, then she would not have been considered cured until she admitted the fact.

George Wells leant forward. "But something has happened to make a difference," he said. "That's why I brought these people to see you. They've seen your cat, been chased by it, in fact."

Agnes looked up, her tired eyes suddenly sparkling. "You've seen it too?" she asked in a relieved whisper.

"Only too clearly," Jill said with a shiver. "The damn thing chased us through the woods and we had to break into your house to get away from it."

"Was it like a big black panther?" asked the old lady, not even bothering with the house breaking confession.

Brian smiled. "The biggest and the blackest cat I've ever seen," he assured her.

Dr Ellis leant back. "So you see, Agnes, the only reason you had to be here was because you were seeing cats nobody thought existed. But if they do, then I can't think of any reason why you should have to stay here. We'll have to go through the paper work of course, as you were committed under the Mental Health Act, but it's only a matter of time before you'll be safely back in your own home."

"Isn't that wonderful?" said Jill with a broad smile. Agnes Briant said nothing; she stared across the room, out of the sunlit window, lost in thought.

George touched her arm. "Do you understand? You can go home."

A tear trickled down the old lady's cheek, running a zigzag path down the grooves of her wrinkled face. "Do I have to go, Doctor?" she asked in a quivering voice after a few minutes silence. "Must I leave here?"

There was a moment of shock. Then Dr Ellis said gently, "Don't you want to go home?"

Agnes shook her head. "I did at first," she said softly. "I desperately wanted to go back to my own house, to be among my own things, my memories. But I don't think I do now." She looked up almost pleadingly. "You see, at home there is no-one to need me, nothing to do. I just potter about, trying to find things to do to fill my time before I die." She looked around the bleak, green-painted, shabby day room. "But here it is different, here I've things to do, people to talk to, people to help." She leant forward and patted the knee of a young woman who had obvious Downs Syndrome features. The girl's face lit up and she beamed at Agnes. "Young Dora, she's not able to read, you know, but I can still read if the print is large enough, and I'm reading Jane Eyre to her, a bit every evening. It's a whole new world to the girl, the world of books. The staff are much too busy to do things like that. And I help feed some of the really disabled ones at meal times and help them get undressed at night." She clutched at the doctor's hand. "Do you see? I can be useful here, help people and in return, I don't feel I've nothing left but my memories. I'm also not lonely, I've people to talk to, if not always the patients, I can chat to the staff."

"You're sure it's not just fear that makes you want to stay?" asked Dr Ellis quietly. "You've been here a few weeks now and hospital is a bit like prison. After a time, the outside world sometimes becomes quite frightening. Patients feel as if they can't cope."

Agnes chuckled. "Are you suggesting I've become institutionalised?" she asked wickedly.

Dr Ellis nodded. "Yes."

"Perhaps, a little," she agreed. "But that is not the reason I don't want to be sent away. I've spent time in hospital in the past and one soon adjusts back to normal life." She shook her head. "No, it really isn't that. If I have to go home, I think I'll just quietly decay and fade away, a bit like Miss Haversham, if you know your Dickens." She looked around her. "Here I've a reason to live, a sort of purpose. Here I can help people, be useful." She looked down at the gaudy knitted squares of the blanket around her legs. "Please, don't send me away to rot and die alone."

Dr Ellis looked at the bent head with its crown of shining grey hair twisted into a knot. "But Agnes, how can I keep you here if you've nothing wrong with you. We know the cat exists, we can't pretend these people are lying."

"I understand that," Agnes murmured. "But being here could have made me mad, you know. Even, if I wasn't mad to start with." She looked hard into Dr Ellis's eyes. He stared back at her, meeting her gaze.

"And just what grounds would I have for considering you're mad?" he asked.

The old lady shut one eye in a definite wink. "Oh, I've been doing a lot of watching and listening since I've been here, Doctor. I think I can persuade you I'm mad, if I really need to." She turned back to Brian and Jill. "It's very kind of you to come and see me like this. Please don't think I'm ungrateful. I really am pleased that somebody else has seen the beast, even if it's only..." She reached across and patted George Wells' arm, "even if it's to prove to this nice young policeman here that I really wasn't just a silly old lady wasting his time."

"I never thought that, not ever," George assured her.

"Ah, but you didn't think there really was a cat, did you?" she asked him, smiling.

George shook his head. "Well no, I must admit I didn't believe there was a cat, but I never thought you were wasting my time. Just mistaken, that's all."

"And now you know I wasn't?"

George leant over to kiss the wrinkled cheek. "And now I know."

She sighed. Not a sad sigh but a relieved one then, closed her eyes. "I really think I need to rest a little now, if you won't think me rude. It's all been a bit tiring, suddenly getting back my mind."

The visitors stood up.

"Of course," said Jill gently. "May we come and see you again?"

Agnes nodded, though her eyes remained closed. "I'd like that. I don't have many visitors, everyone is so far away." She sighed. "And I do so like to see the young people, so full of hope and life." She opened her eyes and smiled up at them. "Next time I'll try not to be so tired." She closed her eyes and sat perfectly still. The others weren't sure if she was just resting or actually asleep. They moved quietly away.

"Fuck off! Pissing know-all doctors," snapped Rosie as they edged past her violently clicking needles. Dr Ellis turned at the door and gave a quick wink at the others before giving the glaring woman a clear two-fingered gesture. Rosie threw back her head and roared, great masculine guffaws of laughter.

"Therapy not in the medical practice books," muttered Dr Ellis with a grin as he shook their hands.

"Effective though," Brian suddenly warmed to the man within the plastic doctor.

"Will you keep Mrs Briant here, if she really doesn't want to go home?" Jill asked the doctor worriedly.

"Too soon to say. If she honestly wants to stay here, well, she's been signed in under the Mental Health Act, so I can just let things remain as they are." He held Jill's hand warmly and she felt a sudden feeling of trust in the man and understood something of his relationship with his patients. "But you know, I think it's a little deeper than that she doesn't want to go home, and if I'm right, then there may even be a solution. She's formed a positive relationship with our Dora, rather like a mother and a daughter. That's why I think she wants to stay."

"Because she won't leave Dora?"

"Exactly. Now we've been thinking for some time about trying Dora out in sheltered accommodation. She's not really mental in the usual sense of the word; she's just slow in taking things in. Had she been born today she would have gone to a special school and realised her full potential. Sadly, forty years ago, people like Dora were just locked away and forgotten."

"So you might let Dora out?" asked George, following the doctor's train of thought.

"Agnes is physically at risk. She does need a little help looking after herself because of her arthritis, whereas Dora can do simple tasks without any problems. She just can't manage without being instructed. Put the two together and I think we could have a perfect working unit."

"So you mean to discharge Dora to live with Mrs Briant?" exclaimed Jill.

"It's worth a thought. It will release two much needed beds here and I think make two ladies very happy."

"I think it's a marvellous idea!" cried Jill, and without thinking, she hugged Dr Ellis.

"Goodness!" exclaimed the doctor as Jill released him from her bear-like embrace. "I wish all my decisions produced such a bonus." He laughed. "Well, I must get on with my work. Thank you for taking the trouble to come here and explain things."

"Just one thing, Doctor," said the policeman in a serious mood.

Dr Ellis paused, "Yes."

"I think before anyone returns to Mrs Briant's house, we must get the place cleaned up and this cat business sorted out. It wouldn't be a good idea to put an old and a disabled lady where there's a risk of a cat attack."

"But the cat never attacked her as I understand it. She just used to see it."

"That's right. But things seem to have changed. For whatever reason, the animal seems to have become more aggressive. It virtually tore Mrs Briant's house apart trying to get to these two here. If the door hadn't held, I reckon we would be dealing with a killer now."

"I think we are anyway," said Brian softly. George Wells raised an eyebrow and looked directly at him but said nothing.

"I think you've got a point," said Dr Ellis cheerfully, missing the exchange of meaningful glances. "No matter though, we'll arrange a sheltered flat as a temporary measure. Well, I must be off. Do keep in touch and let me know how things go." He guided them to the main entrance and then disappeared into the lift with a wave of his hand. They walked into the sunlight towards the parked police car.

"You say we're dealing with a killer?" asked George quietly as he drove through the hospital gates. "Why?"

"I don't know we are. It's just a possibility," said Brian while staring out of the window. The policeman grunted.

"You're thinking of young Andrew Roberts?" he muttered. "I wondered what you two were doing up in Whiteoaks."

"It was Jill who first suspected there might be a connection between Andrew's disappearance and a number of cat sightings," explained Brian. "When she told me, it was a bit of a shock, but whatever way you look at it, the facts seem to fit. The bike slung across the road, the apparent lack of human intervention, the swiftness and silence of the attack, if there was one, but we didn't have any proof."

"So we went up to Whiteoaks to try and find some evidence, something you'd all missed," added Jill almost apologetically.

"I don't think there was a stone left unturned," P.C. Wells said defensively.

"But the whole point is that you were concentrating on the ground. If a cat was involved, it would be up high, overhead in the trees. Did anyone look up?"

The policeman shook his head. "I don't suppose they did, thinking about it. Well, you don't expect to find clues up trees, do you? Especially, when looking for a body."

The rest of the journey was spent in thoughtful silence.

CHAPTER 9

The sun shone warmly, giving a hint of the summer to come. Fresh leaves rustled in a slight breeze as the cat stared unwinkingly down through the dancing shadows to where the young couple lay beneath the ivy-covered trunk of a large oak. It watched with mild interest as the figures below jerked and writhed together.

"Stop it! Someone might see us," giggled the girl, trying unsuccessfully to push away the boy's hands as he pulled her skirt up to her waist.

"There isn't anyone to see," he panted, thrusting his tongue against her teeth, effectively muffling her protests as he forced her lips apart. As she relaxed with a deep sigh, his hands fumbled at her waist, sliding his fingers beneath the elastic of her pants, pulling the silky material downwards.

"No, no, no," the girl moaned as his fingers searched eagerly.

The cat moved along the branch, the shaking of the branches un-noticed by the couple as they thrust against each other in a frenzy of passion.

"We shouldn't," the girl murmured as she pushed his shirt up from his waist, running her hands back down his spine to the curving swell of his hips. His hands clasped her buttocks, pulling her up towards him. He thrust deeply and urgently and the girl gave a sharp cry as she felt his penetration, then the cry changed to a scream.

"What the fucking hell!" The boy paused and, resting on his arms, looked down at the girl beneath him as she screamed again hysterically, her eyes wide with terror. "What's the matter with you, you stupid tart?"

The girl stared over his shoulder, her hands digging into his back with such force that her nails broke the skin, causing beads of blood to mingle with the beads of sweat that clung to his brown back and naked buttocks.

"For fuck's sake, you stupid bitch, what's the matter?"

He never finished the sentence, possibly never even understood what was happening. With a swift spring the cat dropped like a stone from the overhanging branch. As it landed, one large paw side-swiped him across the head, snapping his neck instantly. The warm blood spurted into the girl's face as the dead weight of his body fell across her but her terror was short. The paw raked across her throat, tearing the unprotected flesh wide open.

Within seconds the boy's and the girl's blood mingled and ran together in a scarlet stream on to the green crushed grass. They died, their bodies still united.

The cat crouched down and gave a soft throaty purr. The two cubs appeared in the undergrowth, tiny shadows in their mother's shade. She sniffed their wrinkling noses, smearing the warm blood across their faces. They were ready to understand the flavour of a fresh kill. She showed them how to lap the hot flowing blood, her rasping tongue tearing at the tender flesh, shredding the meat for them to manage with their tiny teeth.

They learnt quickly, instinct taking over from teaching, as they tasted the warm flesh. Their capacity was limited, so their stomachs were soon filled. Their mother ate at leisure, tearing off large chunks of meat and crunching through the light bones. There was no fur or wool to dispose, but she spat out the ripped material of the victims clothing. Within a short time it would have been difficult to recognise the prey as a species. The remains were just a bloody mess of bone and flesh.

A thud sounded behind the cat, and she snarled over her prey as a second cat, the large brown male, pushed through the tangled undergrowth surrounding the clearing. She was angry at the encroachment on her territory and nervous to have him near with her cubs present. If he did not move on, she would be forced to drive him away for the cub's safety. She growled a warning and slammed down her front paw in a furious stamp. He ignored her aggression and bent his head to sniff the steaming meal, licking his lips in anticipation. The female snarled and lashed out with a clawed paw. He eased away and, despite his heavier bulk, let the female dictate the terms of the dinner arrangements. She had made the kill and a quick inspection had assured him there would be more than enough fresh meat for both of them. He snarled back and then settled down patiently to wait his turn, ignoring the cubs that cowered behind their mother. When he had a full belly, he would be ready to travel.

By nightfall, the cats had gone from the clearing, only blood-soaked earth and ripped crimson stained rags provided a hint of the tragedy that had occurred just hours previously with a few splinters of bone and clumps of hair the only clues as to the nature of the prey. Within days even these were scattered and dispersed by smaller carnivores.

It was as if the boy and girl had never existed. They had been completely absorbed by the world of nature.

Without any clues to their disappearance, the couple's families were confused and hurt, accepting the pair had simply run away together. For many years, two mothers waited in vain for the telephone to ring or a knock to explain the runaways.

And had visions of grandchildren they had never met.

* * *

The conversion of P.C. Wells to belief in the existence of big cats roaming Dartmoor was not shared with his senior officers. This fact was quickly brought home to him when he attempted to persuade his superiors of the need for an official hunt.

"You've got to be off your head!" exploded Inspector Brough. "You want me to put armed police on the moors in a bloody cat hunt?"

George Wells held his ground. "Sir, I believe we are faced with a situation involving a serious risk to public safety."

The inspector glared at the constable. "Every drunk driver is a serious risk to public safety. Any arrogant young kid who gets his hands on a powerful motor; legitimate or stolen, is a serious threat to public safety. Are you suggesting we arm the traffic police to deal with the problem of traffic offences?"

The constable stared straight ahead, past his senior officer, to gaze out of the window. "No sir, not traffic offences. But the cat? Yes."

Brough sighed. "Even if a feral leopard does exist on the moors, we have no proof that it is a danger to anything other than the occasional sheep. Could even prove useful in regulating the deer population. I understand that is getting out of control these days."

"It has attacked people, Sir"

"Ah yes. Your reporter friend." The inspector tapped his pen in irritation. "I suppose, constable, you haven't considered just how useful a cat hunt on the moors could prove to your media source. The Roberts boy abduction has given them a taste for fame and fortune. Now they are out of the limelight, a story like this could just get the ball rolling again."

P.C. Wells knew he had lost the argument. His evidence was a rumour, a vandalised house and a few paw prints; his witnesses were a media source, a lady concussed after falling of her horse, a group of children, and an old lady in a mental hospital.

"One of the witnesses is a vet, Sir."

Brough nodded. "And the girlfriend of the reporter, I believe."

George was dismissed. The inspector gazed down at the file on his desk. The case of the missing Roberts boy worried him. Random abduction cases were always the most difficult to solve, but the Roberts case was unusual in that the boy appeared to have been snatched within earshot of witnesses without any sound. No car driving away, no door slamming, no evidence of any kind to suggest the boy's fate - except this 'big cat' theory.

It was ridiculous. However, it might be as well to check out the possibility discreetly, just as a precaution. He pressed the button on his desk.

"Ask Sergeant Pender to come to my office." He leant back in his chair and stared at the picture of the Roberts boy thoughtfully.

* * *

Sergeant Pender drew up and parked alongside the police car that was waiting outside Mrs Briant's house. Two uniformed policemen were standing in the lane, their trousers tucked into heavy duty wellingtons.

"Good morning, Sergeant." P. C. Drew grinned. "At least it's not raining for our little jaunt around the countryside."

Pender nodded. "The exercise will do you both good. Put the roses back into your cheeks after all that driving around town."

"What are we actually looking for?" asked the other constable. "This area was pretty well combed during the Robert's search."

"Just a wild card, lads. Inspector Brough has had a request from a member of the public, worried about the possibility of a four-legged killer roaming around here. It's our job to put that member of the public's mind at ease."

"A four-legged killer?" echoed Drew. "What the hell is it?"

"It's supposed to be a big cat." Pender scratched his chin. "I suspect we might as well be looking for the hound of the Baskervilles. However, it's a few hours out of the office and a nice day, so I'm not complaining." He began to pull on his Wellingtons.

"And if we find a big cat? What are we supposed to do with it?" asked P.C. Greenwell. Sergeant Pender gave him a withering look

"Put a collar and lead on it, lad, and take it back to the station." He laughed at the young policeman's dismayed expression. "There's no big cat out there. This is just a gesture of goodwill. We plod around the countryside for a bit, then go back to the station to report we haven't encountered any man-eating tigers. The big white chief passes on this information to the worried member of the public and they can once again sleep at night." He stood up and locked his car. "Right, sooner we get started, the sooner we'll be back in the station canteen."

The three policemen set off into the trees; the light was fading as they entered the shadows under the leafy canopy. Soon the distant traffic noises faded and the forested world around them appeared primitive and silent. Jokes about predators seemed out of place in the wilderness of their surroundings. It was only too easy to imagine a creature prowling through the undergrowth, sharp in tooth and claw, and hunting for its dinner.

Spring was nearly over and summer just around the corner. The area had almost recovered from the onslaught of the Roberts search. The torn ground was green with new growth, trampled grass disguised the red earth, the men's weight pressing down on the fragile blades, had crushed them back into the soft mud. The glades were a sea of bluebells, their slender stems dipping with the curling blossoms, the green fruiting hearts pushing apart the darkening blue petals. Violets carpeted the hollows beneath the tree roots and fading clumps of anemones provided splashes of silvery light in contrast to the rich green-blues of the ground cover.

Nature had recovered from the ravages of winter and man.

Drew paused and looked around him, "It's a bit spooky in here," he remarked breathlessly.

Greenwell peered through the seemingly endless rows of trees and bushes. "It's hard to believe we are so close to civilisation," he muttered.

Sergeant Pender tapped his shoulder. "Not so hard to believe in roaming big cats when you realise how wild it is up here. Could be a herd of bloody elephants around, for all we would know."

Drew gave an involuntary shiver. "Shut up, Sarge. You're giving me the willies."

The sergeant gazed across a small clearing. "I'm giving myself the willies," he said with a chuckle. "Come on, lads. We've a fair bit of ground to cover. Let's keep moving."

They had reached the spot where the boy and girl had been attacked, but the passing of weeks had destroyed the evidence, the blood stained earth was now green with fresh growth, the shredded material of their clothing either dispersed on the wind or used by nesting birds and mammals to line their nurseries. Had the policemen known about the tragedy, they might have been able to detect the shards of bone, buttons, and rusting zips that had been rejected by the woodland inhabitants. But they were unaware of the violent deaths that had occurred in the peaceful glade.

One important clue remained. The cat watched the men with interest as they plodded through her territory. Her instinct told her to avoid attacking the group. Unlike sheep, over which she was confident, choosing one individual within the flock, striking her selected prey and ignoring the others, man was a different kind of animal. When she had killed the couple, they had appeared as one animal; it was only after making the kill that she discovered her mistake. She had been lucky then, but she did not want to chance a second multiple attack. The first time she had been so desperate for food, she had attempted to hunt two of the man-prey and between them they had outrun and outwitted her. She did not want to repeat that humiliation. Man was an easy prey only when isolated. She decided to watch and wait.

After three hours of clambering uneventfully around the Devon countryside, the three policemen decided to retrace their steps and call it a day.

"Just to cover more ground, we'll separate here and make our way back to the cars individually," instructed Sergeant Pender.

Sunlight streamed in columns through the gaps in the tree canopy as Drew gazed around him. The woodland no longer looked menacing, it reminded him of picnics as a child. It was the world of Robin Hood and Cowboys and Indians. He smiled to himself. Was what they were doing any different to those distant childhood games? The great white hunter, hunting a big cat.

"How far apart do you want us?" asked Greenwell. Any disquiet they had felt earlier had been dispelled by the uneventful walk.

"Not too far," said the sergeant thoughtfully. "Within hailing distance."

"You don't really believe this big cat story?" asked Drew. Pender shook his head.

"Nothing like that, lad. But it's easy to get lost in these woods. If we stay within vocal range, there will be no chance of me having to send out another search party looking for you two." He grinned. "Very embarrassing to have to send out police searching for the police."

The officers spread out in a line and started back, Pender, who was the more experienced, kept the central point, the two constables flanking him on either side.

The men were walking alone.

The cat made her choice. She padded quietly at the rear, wriggling under the lower branches to avoid making a sound. Her intended prey was less careful, crashing through the tangled undergrowth, branches twanging and snapping as he pushed his way through the overgrown trees. She wrinkled her nose, scenting the air. Her tail lashed from side to side as she suppressed a low growl of anticipation. Soon she would feed.

Sergeant Pender was thinking of his dinner, the fresh air and exercise had given him a healthy appetite. He was quite pleased with himself; the younger men had not coped as well with the long hike. For all three of them the walking became almost hypnotic, a plodding routine, heading home.

No one heard the crash as Drew hit the ground, the soft mud muffling the sound. They were almost out of the woods when Sergeant Pender noticed the absence of noise from the direction

Drew should have been taking. He paused and listened. He could hear Greenwell puffing and panting as he slipped and slithered down the bank leading to the path. But from Drew's direction there was nothing.

Damn! The dozy sod must have veered off route. He waited for Greenwell to join him and together they strained to detect distant movements of Drew fighting his way through the bushes. Only birdsong could be heard, with the distant hum of traffic. There was no sound from the third man.

"When did you lose track of him?" asked Greenwell, desperately wanting to head for civilisation and the police canteen.

Sergeant Pender shook his head. "I don't rightly know." He felt a pang of guilt. While deep in his thoughts, he had lost all track of the others. He had no idea exactly when Drew had taken the wrong direction. He knew he should have noticed the sounds becoming fainter and immediately rectified the situation. He had not done his duty and now he had to sort out the mess. He just hoped that Drew would continue in the right direction to reach the road, for if he went in a circle, he would end up lost on the moor itself.

"What do we do, Sarge?"

"Wait," said Pender shortly. "We bloody well wait."

* * *

It was dark before the alarm was sounded. Inspector Brough was not amused that a discreet recci had ended in a major search for a missing police constable.

"If he took the wrong route, where the hell could he be now?" he demanded, glaring at Pender. The sergeant shuffled his feet uneasily!

"I don't know, Sir. We attempted to retrace our steps back to the spot where we separated. We shouted till we were hoarse. There was nothing. He's just vanished."

"Men don't just vanish, sergeant." Brough stormed out of his office to face the media. It was not a highlight of his career, especially as he tried to fend off questions asking why the police were there in the forest.

"The men involved were acting on my orders. They were simply checking the area in case we had missed anything in the earlier search."

"What?" asked the reporter. "What could three officers find that hundreds missed in the original Roberts search?"

It was a question that Inspector Brough had no intention of answering. "We received some information from the public that we decided to act on," He said quietly. "It was simply a case of elimination."

"Eliminating what?" persisted the reporter.

"I'm sorry. I cannot give you that information," replied Brough shortly. The rest of the press conference consisted of a description of P.C. Drew, a glowing account of his history in the force and the promise that everything possible was being done to trace his whereabouts. His fate was unknown but conjecture was that he had taken a wrong path and met with an accident. The moors were notorious for hidden dangers; he could have fallen and hit his head, wandered into one of the infamous bogs, or simply have been taken ill.

No one, least of all Inspector Brough, suggested an attack by a wild animal could be the cause of the mystery of the missing policeman.

Once more Dartmoor made the national news. The less serious papers suggested alien abduction as a possible answer. It was not a theory that inspired Brough to action.

It was four days before Police Constable Drew's remains were found and Inspector Brough's worst fears were realised.

The search party almost missed the body. Once again the Devon landscape was ripped apart as bushes were beaten flat and trees stripped of their lower branches during the massive hunt for the missing officer. After the first forty-eight hours had passed without contact, his colleagues rightly feared the worst. Only George Wells, Brian Henderson and Jill Forsythe suspected the truth, and they hoped desperately to be proved wrong. P.C. Wells faced his inspector again and formally requested that a cat attack be considered as a possibility to account for his colleague's disappearance. Although still refusing to accept the cat attack theory, Brough did agree to allow Jill access to the area, following the searchers.

The spot where the attack had taken place was identified on the third day when a ripped and bloodstained wellington boot was found under a bush. Immediately, the area was sealed off, and the forensic boys were called in. They found splashes of dried blood in considerable quantities, confirming the worst, but still no body.

On the fourth day of the search, a young police constable paused to make use of a convenient tree trunk. As he stood relieving himself, he felt water dripping off the upper branches on to his back and neck. He wiped away the moisture with his hand to find it stained pink. He looked up and for a moment was spared the horror to come, the green leaf canopy almost hiding the bloody remains P.C. Drew, wedged in the fork of the oak. Only the dangling broken leg, still wearing a wellington boot, identified the body as human.

The young constable passed out.

* * *

Jill found herself urgently summoned to the scene. The police surgeon had examined the remains from the vantage point of a fireman's ladder, though he had no need to confirm death, for only half the body remained. Jill was asked to examine the scene.

"How much of the body was left?" she asked, trying to detach herself from the reality of the situation.

"Not a lot," remarked the police surgeon coolly." The ribcage, pelvis and backbone were stripped of flesh, there was no viscera, the head, arms and one leg are missing." The doctor's dissociation helped Jill to cope with the vision.

"That is consistent with a leopard attack," she explained calmly. "They kill with a throat bite, rip open the abdomen and gut their prey, usually burying the internal organs under earth or leaves. They then take the gutted carcass up a tree to eat at their leisure."

The surgeon nodded. "That certainly fits the condition of the body." He turned to the senior officers at the scene. "I'll confirm the animal attack theory at the post mortem, but I really do not think we have to look to human agency in this one. Everything the vet here has described fits the scene. It looks as if we have a killer cat on the loose."

Inspector Brough sighed. "But what the hell do we do about it?" Human killers were within his experience, animal killers were not.

* * *

It was only a matter of hours before the media linked the disappearance of Andrew Roberts with the death of P.C. Drew. Although there was still no evidence to prove that Andrew had been the victim of a predator attack, the fact that a killer animal was loose on the moors, and that a policeman had been killed within the area of the child's supposed abduction, was enough. Jill and Brian had agreed to keep their encounter with the cat quiet in a vain attempt to prevent local panic and a second media circus, but within two days the matter was out of control.

Many farmers remembered the 1980's beast hunt by the Royal Marine Commandos and they demanded that the armed specialists should return to the moors to finish the job they had started on Exmoor so many years previously.

Others pointed out that the Marines had failed to catch their quarry the last time, so why should they succeed if they were brought in again? The local Member of Parliament raised a question in the House, requesting immediate protection for his constituents. Mothers walked their children to school in groups, accompanied by armed farmers.

It was a situation that could only end in further tragedy.

The authorities were helpless. They asked for assistance.

Specialist aid.

CHAPTER 10

Brian and Jill were invited to a very private meeting to discuss their experience with the cat. Brian was sworn to secrecy. His loyalties had to be divided, for although he was a journalist, he accepted that public safety had to come first, and his job second.

They arrived at the police headquarters to be met by P.C. George Wells. "I've been instructed to take you upstairs," he said grimly. "At least this time they are taking us seriously."

"It's a pity they didn't listen earlier. That poor copper would still be alive," commented Jill.

"I knew the lad in passing," George said wearily. "I just hope it was quick. We accept we might get attacked by villains in the course of duty - it goes with the job - but not like that." He sighed.

He signed them in at the desk and then led the way through into the rear of the front office, a part of the police station that neither Jill nor Brian had ever seen before. It was a vast modern building, consisting of long winding corridors, and a multitude of small rooms and offices. Everywhere uniformed officers were bustling about, most carrying sheafs of paper or files. Although the cat hunt took precedence, the ordinary work of criminal investigation had to continue, routine matters dealt with and the everyday business of policework carried on. Additional staff had been drafted in from the outlying areas to help, causing congestion in the corridors and overcrowding in the offices.

The constable went ahead of them up the stairs, and as they reached the upper floor offices, it was noticeably quieter than on the lower levels. Inspector Brough was waiting for them; Chief Superintendent Mackay was seated at the desk. Two men not in uniform were also seated; a bearded man in his thirties who did not look like a police officer and a clean-shaven smartly dressed man who did. Sergeant Pender produced chairs for Jill and Brian, before joining George to stand quietly by the door.

The bearded man was Victor Morrison, a cat expert from London Zoo. The other man was not introduced.

Chief Superintendent Mackay wasted no time in opening the proceedings. "I've asked you all to come here to discuss what we should do about this killer cat. I think we are all agreed now that there is one." He looked at P.C. Wells, "I'm just sorry we did not accept the facts earlier. We have lost a good fellow officer in extremely tragic circumstances. It is up to us to see we lose no more, officers or civilians."

Morrison scratched his head. "It has to be a leopard by the description. They don't turn man-killers very often, thank god. But when they do they can be the devil to dispose of."

The unidentified man stared intently at Morrison. "How large a range do they have?" he asked in a quiet cultured voice.

"They can travel over thirty miles in a night," replied Morrison.

"Presumably that is only if they have to hunt over a wide territory?" Morrison nodded. "With the amount of prey available on the moors, it should remain in this area." It was a statement rather than a question.

"We think it's got young." Jill almost whispered the words, feeling out of place in the group.

"Why?" The quietly spoken man did not waste his words on small talk.

"We found small prints when we were tracking the big animal," said Brian.

"Could that explain why it has turned killer?" The man turned to Morrison.

"It's possible. A female with young to support would look for easy prey. It could even be that the victims unwittingly got close to the cubs. Maybe she was not hunting for food but protecting her young."

"I believe you were attacked by the creature," the man said to Brian.

"It stalked us before giving chase. Jill heard it following us, then it broke cover and we were lucky to get away. We certainly weren't near any cubs. It was definitely after us."

"You think it was deliberately hunting you?"

"I've no doubt about it. We were on the menu."

The man turned to Jill. "Why do you believe the small prints were the young of the cat and not simply those of other animals?"

"Well, we can't be absolutely certain. They just looked more like small cat prints than dog or fox."

Mackay looked grim. "Mr Morrison, you have the most knowledge of big cats. Could you map out an approximate territory for us? If we can do a sweep over each section, we should be able to flush it out."

"If it is a female with young," Morrison pointed out," she won't be travelling far, so this is the best time to catch her."

"I am afraid catching her is out of the question, Mr Morrison. The risk to the public is too great. She must be shot."

Morrison sighed. Obviously the killing of the big cat was against his nature, but he accepted it as inevitable. "To be certain of getting her, it would be best to clear all farm stock from the area except one target flock to tempt her into range."

Mackay looked at Brough. "Could that be organised?"

"It might take a while," Brough said as he studied a map of the area. "The farms are pretty scattered around that location and the sheep free graze across the moor. We could at least stop public access to the site and shift most of the sheep."

Mackay nodded. "Do it. See if you can rough out the territory today and notify all the farmers to move their stock. It might be as well to put a marksman with the farmers when they are bringing the sheep out, just as a precaution."

"I'd like to have a chat with you two," the quiet man said to Brian and Jill.

"Mr Brown here is a marksman. He will be in charge of the shooters," Mackay informed Brian sharply as the reporter looked at the man with interest.

"You are the only people who can estimate its size and speed," explained Brown. "A cat is a difficult target at the best of times. The more information we have, the better our chances."

"You have hunted big cats before?" asked Jill.

"I have hunted most animals," said Brown with a faint smile. "Including cats."

* * *

It was only later, when they were alone, that Brian voiced his suspicions.

"What did you think of Brown?"

"The big white hunter?" Jill shrugged. "I don't like people who kill for sport."

"I think Brown kills for more than sport," said Brian softly. "I think they've recruited the best." Jill looked at him. "I don't give much for the cat's chances this time," he added. "Not if Brown is who I think he is."

* * *

Brian Henderson had secured a deal with the police. He would remove his reporter's hat on a temporary basis if he were allowed exclusive access to the hunt. It was really a *fait accompli*. He was already so deeply involved that he could cause problems if he published what he knew. Mackay, after consultation with the big chiefs, made him an offer. He could cover the hunt as the official reporter if he agreed to publish nothing till the situation was resolved. However, there were some conditions. Certain facts about the operation would not be made public, even after the event. The police would vet the story before publication. Brian guessed which parts he would not be allowed to report and he agreed, considering it a censorship that made sense.

It took forty-eight hours to clear the moorland site. Jill was appointed the veterinary consultant, Morrison the big cat expert. Brown remained quietly in the background, but everyone involved noticed that when Brown made a suggestion, everyone, even Mackay, jumped.

There was little doubt who was in actual charge of the operation.

A news conference was held without Brown present. Morrison was introduced as adviser to the operation and the public were warned to keep away from the area until further notice. When asked what the plan was, Mackay informed the media that police marksmen were going to encircle the area where the cat was suspected to be. A drive would push through, and the cat would be shot when it broke cover. If the first sweep failed, then a second one would be organised and the operation would continue until successful.

Not even supporters of the Animal Rights campaign objected to the intention to shoot the cat. The death of the policeman, and the possible fate of Andrew Roberts had stilled any thoughts of cuddly fluffy pussycats. No one knew or cared why the cat had been driven to become a man-killer, it had declared war on humans, and it was a war the cat could not win.

* * *

The day of Operation Cat began for the hunters before dawn. At four in the morning Brian and Jill were waiting nervously at Jill's cottage when they heard a Landrover pull up outside. Wrapped up against the chill of the night air, they left the cheerful glow of the warm, brightly-lit house for the still darkness of the early hour. The dog watched them depart before settling back to snooze on the sofa. If humans wanted to go for a walk in the middle of the night, then it was their choice. He would remain and guard the house.

Jill and Brian walked down the path to the army Landrover, wishing they could remain in the warm cottage with the dog. If the countryside had appeared sinister during the day, at night, in the dark, it was positively terrifying. Only the hoot of a distant owl sounded, a reminder that the dark was the time for the hunters to be abroad.

"Good morning. I've been instructed to collect Mr Henderson and Miss Forsythe. I presume that's you two?" A very large man stood by the vehicle. He was dressed in army camouflage, a dark woollen hat pulled down over his ears, only his eyes and teeth gleaming in the darkness. Jill nodded. He opened the door of the battered Landrover. "My name's Broadwood. Sergeant-major Broadwood. I'm running the field operation today."

"Not Mr Brown?" asked Jill.

Broadwood grinned. "Oh, Mr Brown is the boss, madam. But it's me and my lads who get our hands dirty. Shall we go?" Jill and Brian climbed into the vehicle, instinctively obeying a man who was used to being obeyed.

Broadwood squeezed his massive frame into the driving seat, seeming to spread and fill the vehicle. He was conscious of his size and the effect it had on people, and had learnt that by sitting and therefore reducing his height, he could put people at their ease more quickly.

However he also knew when to remain standing as many a poor squaddy could testify.

As they bumped and rattled down the potholed lane, the sergeant-major shouted above the roar of the engine. "I understand you were convinced something like this would happen."

"We knew a killer cat was out there. It had a go at us and we think it was responsible for the Roberts kid disappearing."

"You claim to have seen the animal, I believe."

"Seen it and nearly been killed by the bloody thing!"

Broadwood sighed. "Well now, I must admit I find it very hard to believe in this monster stalking the moors, but on the other hand something attacked and killed that copper, and having looked at the medical report on what was left of the body, it's unlikely the attacker was human. So we should have a fun day."

"Where are we meeting up?" asked Brian, fascinated by the sergeant major. He was reminded of a Boys Own comic book hero.

"On the moors. No point in hanging around the town with a bunch of civvies. We are rendezvousing with the police and my lads at the starting point." He glanced towards them. "I believe you think we are dealing with two separate animals - that right? I would like to be sure on that point before putting my lads in the field."

"Why? What does it matter how many cats there are?" asked Jill irritably. She was feeling the chill of the early morning, and she was afraid. She kept remembering the ferocity of the creature that had chased them.

Brian put his arm around her and felt her shivering. He understood, sharing her memories. "Descriptions of the cats vary in colour. Some people claim to have seen a big brown cat, others a jet black animal."

Jill felt ashamed of her rudeness. "I'm sorry," she said, "Just thinking about it brings back the terror." She paused. "We think there might be cubs."

"Is it mum or dad we are after?"

"Mum. The one that chased us was definitely female."

"Well, maternal instinct no doubt accounts for her behaviour. I need to know if we are up against one or two killers." He stared at the blackness beyond the headlight beam. "I have the safety of my men to consider. If we are dealing with just one killer animal, fine. We stake out and when we spot the target - bang! End of cat. However, if more than one animal is around, then we could have real problems. While the lads have one cat in their sights, another could have the lads in its, so to speak. The only deaths we want up on the moors are those connected with four-legged carcasses, not two."

After a brief pause, Brian said: "I take your point. But, while I think there might be more than one big cat up there, it's the black one that's the killer, I'm sure of it."

"And the brown one is not big enough to be a lion, so, if it exists, then it must be a puma, which makes all the difference," added Jill. "Pumas aren't usually dangerous to man, but the black one has to be a melanistic leopard, and that would be dangerous even without cubs."

"Why?"

"A leopard eats monkeys and apes."

"So we look like dinner?" Broadwood suggested with a grin.

"Exactly. The brown one should be relatively harmless."

"To be on the safe side, I'm afraid that anything resembling a big cat will be a target. I just hope we get a clean shot at the beast. Cats are very difficult to kill due to their muscular build and gait. Often in hunting big cats, the bullet will rip through the muscle without killing the creature."

"You've hunted big cats before?" asked Brian.

Broadwood gestured. "My field is weapons, my interest guns. Yes, I've hunted most big game throughout the world. That's why they assigned me to this one. Although the prey I'm trained to hunt is the two-legged variety. They are the most dangerous kind." As if he had said too much, he stopped talking and concentrated on his driving. The vehicle jerkily bumped and bounced along the rough lanes. "Sorry about the noise," he shouted above the combined roar of the engine and the howl of the exhaust. "It's the only one I can drive in reasonable comfort as they've moved the seat back for me."

"I thought the army maintained all their vehicles," Brian shouted back.

"Our vehicles are like us," was the bellowed retort. "Well used, a bit rusty round the rivets, but with good guts!"

His howl of laughter deafened them. Giving up any form of conversation over the scream of the engine, the two passengers hung desperately on to their seats as they rattled along the rutted moorland tracks. Broadwood might be a good hunter, but they decided his driving techniques left a lot to be desired.

The sky was tinged with rose as the cold dawn began to light the landscape. As they reached a cattle grid, leading on to the moor itself, a torch beam flashed. Coming to a halt, they were confronted by a uniformed policeman waving them down.

"Are you authorised to go on to the site, sir?" he asked.

Broadwood waved an identification pass at him. "We are expected. My lads are already up there."

"I don't think they've arrived yet, sir. I would have seen them pass," said the policeman.

"You wouldn't," shouted the sergeant major as the Landrover once more roared into action, leaving the bewildered policeman in a spray of mud and exhaust fumes. "If my lads couldn't walk past a civvy roadblock without being spotted, I'd kick their arses from John O'Groats to Land's End!" he yelled cheerfully.

"Where are we going?" bellowed Brian.

"We think we've mapped out the area where the animal is laying up. Mind you, that still leaves a good few miles of forestry and rough to cover, but at least we haven't got to seal off the whole of the moors. That would be a problem."

The Landrover suddenly spun off the track and turned through a farm gate to shudder to a stop in a large field. Brian and Jill looked around them, amazed.

"Anyone would think we were at war!" exclaimed Jill.

"We are," said Broadwood dryly as he unravelled himself from behind the steering wheel. The field around them was filled with uniforms. Men in combat gear, their faces blackened, rifles cradled lovingly in their arms or slung across their backs, were sitting or standing in small groups. In the centre of the field stood a hastily erected tent, marked by a staked wooden plaque as Field Operations Headquarters. Outside the tent a mixed group of local farmers, police officers and army territorials were gathered. It was painfully obvious that the professional soldiers were remaining apart from the rest of the assembly.

The sergeant major strode across to the group by the tent, with Brian and Jill breaking into a trot to keep up with him.

"Good morning gentlemen. I see my men have arrived." Broadwood glanced at the pale sky. "Well, shall we get on with it? The sooner we start, the sooner we finish." He looked at the mixed group. "Now it seems this animal counts us as part of its menu, so that makes it highly dangerous. So if anyone is harbouring any ideas about being kind to dumb animals, forget it! This is a very dangerous pussycat, with a liking for human flesh."

"Thanks for the pep talk," muttered one of the policemen. "Speaking personally, I prefer dogs anyway."

"Now, as some of you already know, there may be additional complication," added Broadwood.

"Do we really need anything more than a fucking great killer cat on the loose?" remarked a civilian sarcastically.

"We might have two," announced Broadwood grinning. "We don't know for certain but we could be dealing with two different animals. It doesn't make any difference. Anything resembling a cat is a target." He glanced at a farmer who was clutching his shotgun and looking a little sick. "Are all the civvy guns good shots?" he asked.

The farmer nodded. "The best around here."

"Good. We don't want any idiot blasting off and shooting us up the arse," Broadwood stated shortly. He opened out a large map of the area and spread it over the bonnet of a nearby car. "You can see the areas of forestry that we have marked off. All these areas are possible denning areas for the beast and we are going to work our way systematically through the lot."

A farmer whistled. "That's a fair bit of ground to cover."

"So we work fast. The plan is that we'll start in the area of the attack, as it is possible the policeman stumbled upon the cat's home territory. All of the local guns will ring each section and we will work our way through to meet up with them, hopefully flushing anything out ahead of us. Now, unless you get a good sight on the cat, don't any of you fire, and don't shoot at anything else. You're not here to clear the area of vermin, and a shot that kills a fox could make the cat double back and, with the density of the forest, it could get back past us. It must feel that the way ahead is safe and the danger lies behind it."

"Suppose it doesn't run?" asked one of the professionals. He had approached so quietly that the others had not noticed him join them. "It might hold its ground."

Broadwood's response was instantaneous. "That's why we are going in, corporal. We're too tough for it to eat!" Laughter broke the tension. "Tell the lads to go in quietly. Once in position, they can make as much noise as they like - but watch overhead. This baby is going to be as at home up in the trees as on the ground, and we don't want anyone wearing leopard skin hats."

The corporal nodded and moved away as silently as he had arrived. Jill was reminded of a cat. Broadwood continued to outline the plan of action.

"The important thing for the outside guns is, don't shoot us! You'll hear us coming, but only shoot if the cat breaks cover and you've got a clear line of vision. Everyone clear?"

Nods of agreement assured him. He turned to Brian. "Although the civvy and the police guns are staying outside, if you've no objections, I'd like you in the trees with me. You're the only person here to have actively trailed the beast, and you might spot something the rest of us could miss. You also know its tracks."

"Okay."

"I'd like you, Miss Forsythe, to stay with the ring, just in case someone does get the chance of a shot. I'm afraid you are our token vet to keep the cruelty to dumb animals crowd happy. You understand that?" Jill nodded. He folded the map. "Right, let's go!"

Without warning the sergeant-major suddenly boomed across the field and the listeners discovered that the big man had an even bigger voice, the civilians getting the impression of the parade ground sergeant-major that the soldiers knew only too well. "Right, you dozy lot of girls. Move out!"

Silently, without a murmur, his men picked up their gear, shouldered their packs and moved forward in a neat orderly line, their rifles cradled across the fronts of their bodies, at the ready for instant action. The men were working in small teams, each group equipped with a radio linking them both to the police and the sergeant major. Brian gave Jill a quick squeeze on the arm before walking after Broadwood, though to catch up with the big man's long stride, he had to increase his gait to a steady trot. Within minutes the soldiers had filed through the gate and were out of sight, leaving the field looking strangely empty, despite the fifty or so farmers, police officers (including Brough and Pender), the group of part-time soldiers and Jill and Morrison.

"How long will it take to get around the woods?" asked Jill, feeling rather lonely without Brian.

Inspector Brough looked up. "They should be in position and start moving through in about thirty minutes. They'll radio us before they start to push forward. If you'll excuse me for a moment, I'll get our group into their positions and then I'll be back."

Taking the map, he called the various scattered groups towards him and showed them their positions. Soon most of the men had moved off in threes and fours, each group carrying a small radio. "Now, remember, only shoot if it's a clear view of the cat. If you see or hear anything suspicious, radio in."

Within fifteen minutes there was only a small group left in the field consisting of Brough, a couple of territorial soldiers, Sergeant Pender, two police constables, Morrison and Jill.

Brough looked around. "Well, I suppose we'd better get into our own position." He looked at Jill. "We have organised it rather well, I think. No wet ditches for us. We've got the comfort of the police van."

"But doesn't that mean we'll miss out if anything comes?" asked Jill, rather disappointed.

He smiled. "No, we'll be in contact with all the units, plus having a view across the next field to the edge of the wood. If anything happens, we'll know it immediately and we can reach all units within minutes. In the meantime, however, we can have a peaceful cup of instant coffee while we await developments."

On the other side of the wood Brian was being offered no such creature comforts. Puffing and panting, he waded after Broadwood, amazed that such a big man could move so silently at such speed. Broadwood was in his element, his own world. Talking to civilians and making polite conversation with other people's women, he was abrupt and clumsy, but in the open air, the wilderness, with his own men, he came into his own. Brian could understand why he was chosen for the task ahead. He moved swiftly and silently, positioning his men with calm authority, and they obeyed every gesture without a sound. Brian had the feeling he was watching a silent movie or the television with the sound turned down. Without a word being spoken, each man slipped quietly into position until there was an even line of guns stretching a third of the way round the wood. Beyond the last man at either end of the line they knew the farmers and the police were in hidden positions, fingers itchy on the triggers, all waiting, some feeling nervous, others excited.

Unlike the professionals. To a man, they seemed calm and unbothered, treating the whole operation as if it were a routine exercise. Brian felt complete admiration for their professionalism. Despite his own unease at the prospect of meeting up with the killer beast, he felt secure in their presence - a security that was needed. With a wave from Broadwood, as one man, the whole line stepped out of the sunlight into the cool darkness of the forest.

The first sweep was under way.

CHAPTER 11

For the first few yards under the trees the soldiers slipped silently forward, not even betraying their presence by the cracking of a twig beneath their heavy boots. Then, just as Brian was marvelling at how so many men could move so quietly, it all changed. Brian presumed that the sergeant major had given a signal which he had missed because, all at once, the men lost their stealth and crashed and blundered forward with a cracking of branches and a chorus of shouts and piecing whistles.

"Make as much noise as you can," shouted Broadwood, an instruction that Brian felt somewhat unnecessary, acutely conscious as he was of the noise he had already been making. "If the bastard's in here, we want to make sure it hears us."

They stumbled and bellowed their way through the tangled conifers, the springy branches whiplashing back across their arms and unprotected faces, causing some of the yells and curses to be genuine cries of pain. Deeper and deeper into the trees they moved, the line across unbroken, edging its way slowly forward. Brian looked around in the gloom, it was hard to believe that the sun was shining outside the shady world of spiny-fingered trees, that beyond the flattened sheltering branches, birds were singing and lambs bleating in search of their grazing mothers. Suddenly there was a moment of excitement as something crashed through the branches ahead to the right of them. Everyone froze and listened intensely but the sounds were caused by a nervous pigeon, flapping clumsily through the upper branches.

The line started once again to move relentlessly forward, and Brian almost tripped over a length of red and white tape that was stretched around a break in the trees. It was seconds before he realised it was police marker tape and was obviously indicating the place where the policeman's body had been found. He shivered and wondered what the man who had died in this dark and dismal site had been like.

Broadwood noticed Brian's reaction. "That's where they found the body," he shouted. "I doubt the beast will still be in this area. Too much police activity over the last few days, but we had to start somewhere and I decided we'd get this bit over with first. Bit morbid, isn't it? Thinking about that poor bloody copper. What a way to go?"

Brian nodded, although he felt the word morbid was not quite expressive enough.

Outside in the sunlight, the only excitement for the waiting trigger fingers was the terrified passage out into the open of two roe deer that crashed, panic-stricken, out of the forestry plantation and almost leapt over one of the gun positions in their flight. As time passed, the groups outside the trees heard the shouts and yells of the beaters getting louder and louder. Finally, the unmistakable bellow of Sergeant-major Broadwood filled the air.

"Do us a favour and keep those fingers off the triggers. We're coming out!"

"Standby! They're coming out!" was relayed over the radio to all positions. Someone shouted the all clear to the trees. Suddenly, without any noticeable movement, the trees became men and the soldiers stepped out of the gloom into the bright light.

There was a short break for lunch. Broadwood spent the time studying the map with the senior police officers and Morrison. "Okay, move out everybody! Position two!" bellowed the dulcet tones of the sergeant major, before he turned to Morrison. "As we thought, a blank. My money's still on position three."

"Why three?" asked Brian, bringing up the rear of the group.

Broadwood flexed his massive shoulders. "If you look on the map," - he opened it out and spread it across the Landrover - "you can see I've marked all known incidents and a few of the suspected ones. They form quite a distinct circle, a possible hunting territory. Slap bang in the centre is the largest area of forestry, and it's my bet that is where the beast dens up."

Brian peered at the markings. "It makes sense," he agreed.

"But if you think that's where it is, why didn't you start looking there?" asked Jill curiously. "I'll agree that it looks the best area."

"Unfortunately we must work a pattern, a system, no matter what our hunches," explained Broadwood. "So we work our way across the board, even if my money is on that wood. That's where I think we'll get results."

The sweep through position two, an identical operation to the first, also drew a blank, apart from half a dozen terrified roe deer and a very insecure looking fox, which owed its continued existence to Broadwood's firm orders that no shot be fired at anything but a cat. Its russet form slithered into the surrounding undergrowth, past itching enemy fingers, unaware that its life had been spared by the presence of a rather large feline.

The surrounding wilderness had often taken human life; its danger was part of its beauty, and over the years a considerable number of hikers and hillwalkers had set off across the misty hills to their deaths. Legends of great black hounds and deep moorland bogs that could swallow the unwary traveller - man, horse and cart - without a trace were common. The possibility of a big cat being loose aroused more emotion in the sheep rearing community, but even that was more a matter for healthy argument than actual fear.

Private opinion among some of the farmers was that the cat was a fantasy, a killer dog a possible reality. Even among the police a good proportion were of the same opinion, one or two querying the forensic evidence that no human agency was involved in the death of P.C. Drew.

As the day wore on and the guns took up their agreed positions for the third sweep, a number of the civilians relaxed, believing that the whole exercise was a complete waste of time and money. Neighbours lit up the cigarettes and chatted to each other, guns were no longer clutched at the ready. The atmosphere was no longer tense.

On the far side of the wood the mood was very different. The professionals did not expect immediate results and they had learned patience. All had trained as snipers and had been taught that long hours spent motionless up a tree or half-buried in a ditch was the name of the game. You didn't relax, ever, not in the field. Every branch crackle, every fluttering bird was suspect, every sense was tuned in to expect the unexpected. Slowly, calmly, the line steadily moved forward. The only uncharacteristic aspect of military behaviour was that everyone made as much noise as possible. To men trained to stealth, even in the surroundings of the British countryside, this felt dangerously wrong, contrary to all their beliefs, all their training. Brian found himself trailing slightly behind Broadwood, his legs, unaccustomed to such prolonged and strenuous exercise, were aching unbearably, his calf muscles feeling knotted and cramped. He deeply regretted the years spent sitting on his well-padded backside, driving short distances around town. He knew it wasn't the years that caused the trouble - Broadwood proved that - it was the continued misuse of his body.

Section three was the largest area of woodland so far covered and moving slowly and cautiously, listening every few yards for any movement ahead, was time consuming. While those outside the forestry plantation relaxed, thought about cups of refreshing tea, consuming a pint down at the local or, bored, simply dozed in the sunshine, the soldiers moved relentlessly forward, ignoring the passing hours. Eventually their shouts grew louder as they neared the outer edge of the trees and the farmers and police stirred themselves.

Brough scanned the open ground with binoculars. "Well, if anything is going to come out, it should be soon," he remarked. The long wait had removed even his edge and the whole operation began to feel like routine. Jill squinted into the sun and wondered where Brian was.

He was at that moment rubbing a bruised skin, having tripped rather heavily over a tree root.

"Hell!" he exclaimed ruefully. Broadwood suddenly waved him to silence. As a man, the guns ceased all movement and sound, the forest became suddenly deathly silent. The sergeant major signalled to the left and everyone listened intently. Something reasonably large was moving ahead of them, they could hear the crack of branches and the sound of breathing.

"A deer?" whispered Brian, but Broadwood shook his head.

"Listen to the branches, just an odd one cracking every so often. That means whatever it is, it's below the main growth, it's fairly low to the ground and missing all but the lowest branches, but it's bigger than something the size of a fox that would miss them out altogether. No, it's large but smaller than a deer, and low moving. This could be our baby!" He spoke quietly into the radio.

Brough leapt as the radio suddenly cracked into life.

"Something large but not deer, moving our way about two o'clock to your position."

Something is happening!" the inspector shouted to the others. He flicked the radio switch. "Stand by all positions. Something is moving our way at two o'clock."

The circle of guns began to concentrate again on the edge of the wood, the adrenaline starting to flow. Could this be it? They waited expectantly. The sound of raised voices started in the wood and the professionals again moved forward. A couple of wood pigeons suddenly flapped out, squawking in terror, but significantly perhaps, no deer appeared. The soldiers continued their steady progress towards the edge of the trees, the waiting guns and sunlight. They began to chant, slapping their hands in rhythm against the butt of their riffles. The effect was rather like a Zulu war chant.

Ahead of them the black cat paused, uncertain in which direction the greatest danger lay. There was no blind panic in her movements. She waited in the last trees, snarling silently as she sniffed the air, assessing the situation. Whatever was behind her smelt of man but was not behaving as the man animal should; ahead was an even stronger man scent. The cat made her decision. Her two cubs were sleeping in the fork of a tree, hidden from view. She had to lead the danger away from her family. With bunched muscles she launched herself out into the open, away from the protection of the trees.

"Christ! Look at that thing move!"

With open mouths, the civilian guns watched as the huge black cat streaked across the field towards them.

"Fire, damn you! Fire!" howled Brough over the radio, but the three men directly in the path of the speeding cat had other ideas. The first shock of actually seeing the animal now gave way to fear. The cat was travelling straight for them at the speed of an express train. To farmers, lacking the training of professionals, it seemed a good idea to move themselves, though a slightly lesser pace was the maximum they could manage. With a yell, they legged it in different directions, obstructing the line of fire for other guns overlooking the area and leaving the way clear for the cat to break through the ring and make good her escape.

A few token shots from other positions followed the bounding black form as it reached cover.

As suddenly as it had started, the whole incident was over. It had taken less than thirty seconds. The soldiers came charging out of the trees, alerted by the shots, but only an empty clearing greeted them. The cat was away. Broadwood guessed what had happened.

"Oh, shit" he exclaimed as he stood blinking in the sunlight, but there was nothing he could do, even if his men had been in time to sight the animal, there was no way they could have discharged their rifles in the direction of the civilian population.

Inspector Brough put his head in his hands. He forgot Jill's presence when he announced with great feeling, "Fuck!"

There was no help for it, they had to start all over again.

CHAPTER 12

Broadwood stretched out his long legs and gazed miserably at his muddy boots. "It's my fault. I should have left some of my lads outside the wood. You can't blame civvies for losing their nerve when faced with something like that coming at them."

The group was seated in the cramped conditions of the mobile headquarters, the van made even smaller by Broadwood's massive frame. Brough looked strained and tired. He had not slept well since Drew's death, for which he felt personally responsible. With all his many years in the force, his gift for administration, and his high rank, he had never before lost a man on duty. Logically, he knew that no one could have predicted the killing. He had not sent the man alone into the area and there had been no actual proof of the cat's existence, only a few garbled accounts from so-called eyewitnesses. Still, if he had paid more attention to their stories, even considered the possibility of danger to the public, Police Constable Drew would now be safely home with his family, not a mangled corpse with only DNA as a means of formally identifying it. Brough was not sure he would ever sleep peacefully again now that they knew a killer beast was loose, and he shuddered at the thought of more half-eaten bodies wedged up trees.

"It wasn't your fault. I should have put more experienced men in the field," he said to the army sergeant major. "I never anticipated the speed or power of the creature. Even though I was waiting for it, the actual sight of the thing was totally unexpected."

Morrison smiled. He was the only one present who did not seem in awe of the creature. He loved the big cats. He respected them, understood them, and was not afraid of them. To the others the cat was a demon, an evil killer; to him the cat was simply living normally. It was hungry, so it hunted. There was no malice or wickedness in its behaviour. It was simply surviving in an alien environment.

"What a magnificent animal! Its lame, you know. Must have injured its back leg at some time," he said enthusiastically. "Probably why it's been attacking humans. If the injury was recent, it would have had to hunt easy prey for a while."

Brian looked at him. "Are you telling us that thing was moving slowly?" he asked.

Morrison scratched his head thoughtfully. "Well, I'd say it had adjusted to using three legs, but that must have slowed it down a certain amount. Has to, if you think about it."

"How do you know it was injured?" asked Jill. "It's looked pretty healthy each time I've seen it, and I didn't notice it limping."

"Oh, it wouldn't limp, not in the accepted sense. Not once it had adjusted." Morrison waved his arms in a fluid movement. "It's simply a matter of rhythm. If you are familiar with the flow of feline movement, you can detect any deviation in the gait."

Brough cut short the lecture abruptly. "Why it's a killer doesn't concern me. Only how we take it out before it kills anyone else."

"I think we can all agree on that." Broadwood rubbed his stubby chin ruefully. "At least, we have a clearer picture now of what we are up against. Unfortunately, I didn't get a good look at the thing! Just a glimpse of the back end."

Jill sighed. "When it chased us, we didn't really see it properly, but today, watching it bound across that field, I thought it looked beautiful. It's a shame it has to be killed."

"Don't feel too sad," muttered the sergeant major with a boyish grin. "We've got to get it first, and so far the points are all on the cat's side, not ours."

"We have to get it before there are any more deaths." The inspector spoke sharply, not seeing any humour in the situation.

Jill looked at Morrison. "I suppose there's no chance that it will leave humans alone, now it has recovered from its injury?" she asked hopefully.

"It's possible, of course… but doubtful. Once it has found an easy prey, why should it go back to working harder for its supper?"

They sat quietly for a few minutes, the animal lovers among them torn in loyalties, the others simply worried by the enormity of the problem facing them. Broadwood finally broke the silence.

"How soon could we clear this area of all humans and farm stock?" he asked Brough.

"Depends on what you mean by area. If you just mean taking a wider sweep beyond the wood, not long. If you're thinking about clearing a large area of moorland, it's doubtful if we could. Too many scattered farms."

The sergeant major grunted. "I'll settle for a couple of miles radius of the wood being cleared of farm stock, and all civilians within range told to stay indoors."

"As most of the local farmers were here today, I don't think they will take a lot of persuading," Brough said.

Broadwood heaved himself up. "Then do it. My men can help you. Get the farmers to shift all stock off these hills for the next forty-eight hours." He turned. "Oh, except for one. I want just one sheep left. Preferably a vocal one."

Morrison grinned. "A stake-out," he murmured. "Our best chance."

* * *

The area was cleared within twenty-four hours. After just a fleeting view of the beast, the local farmers gave their full co-operation in moving their stock. They also needed no persuasion to agree to remain in their homes.

The following evening, the trap was set. As the sun slowly sank below the horizon, touching the hilltops with a copper glow, Broadwood, Brian, Jill and Morrison were again gathered in the confines of the mobile unit. Brough had decided to take personal charge of the roadblocks but was keeping in constant touch with the others by radio. He had to be certain that no outsiders could stray into the field of fire. The possibility of civilians getting shot was more terrifying to those operating in both forces than the chance of the cat killing again.

Outside the van a dozen solders were relaxing, some cleaning their weapons, other stretched out on the grass, their berets pulled over their eyes, apparently dozing. A couple of police officers were standing talking, appearing out of place and ill at ease in the presence of the military. Because of the intended use of firearms in a public area, the police had to be present. Only the three civilians had slept for a few hours, the others all looked tired. It had been a hard day organising the clearance of the area.

"How can we be sure it will still be here?" asked Jill.

"We can't," replied Broadwood shortly. "But Morrison is the cat expert, and he thinks it will hang around this area."

Morrison looked uncomfortable. "I'm not sure, but it's worth a try. Most animals, especially cats, have a territory and this wood appears to be the central point in this one's patch."

"We know how close we came to getting the bugger, but the cat doesn't," added Broadwood, speaking directly to Jill. "We were just a minor disturbance to it. Remember, if it did attack the Roberts boy, then despite all the police activity in the area, it stayed its ground. It was certainly there when you were. There seems to have been a history of sheep killing round here, so we can assume before it added us to its menu, then lamb chops were the thing. According to Morrison, if it hasn't killed since the attack on the copper, it should be getting hungry. So presumably it will be out hunting tonight."

"And with the stock shifted, you think it will go for the bait animal?" asked Brian.

"Makes sense," said Broadwood. "We've run the local hunt hounds through the wood to flush out any deer, so food in there should scarce. One solitary ewe must make a prime target for it, if it is still around."

"Wouldn't the cat have been flushed out by the dogs?"

"It's more likely to have gone up a tree," said Morrison. "I gather the dogs were a bit reluctant to go in, which would suggest the cat was around this morning."

"The poor little bastards were scared shitless. We had to drag them through one part of the plantation," Broadwood added.

Which part?" asked Brian.

Broadwood pointed out of the window, towards the bleating ewe. "That patch over there. That's why we've staked out this spot." He looked at his watch. "Time to make a move, I think. I want the lads in position before it gets dark."

He stepped outside into the golden glow of the sunset and gave a single long whistle. At once the men gathered up their gear and without a word, moved off in pairs across the field to their pre-selected positions. Within minutes only the two policemen remained. Broadwood turned to them.

"Right. My lads will be in position now. I'd like you two to park about half-a-mile down the road. Make quite sure no one can reach us from that direction. Remain there until one of my lads comes to get you. Don't come back without hearing from us, not even if you hear rifle fire. If the cat breaks through the positions, my lads will have to take it from behind. You will be in direct line of fire if you move out of the shelter of the hill. So you must stay put until you get the all clear."

The policemen nodded. They had seen what had been left of their colleague and had no desire to be shot or eaten. As they drove off across the field, Broadwood looked at the darkening sky.

"Okay," he murmured to the others, "I suggest you all stretch your legs for a few minutes, then we get settled in. Noise must be kept to the minimum, so don't get tempted into any cosy chats. You'd be surprised how far voices travel at night. And if any of you smoke, tough! The lads are staked out to cover a fairly wide area, with luck they'll spot it before it even has a chance to strike."

Obediently the group stepped out into the warm rays of the setting sun, feeling the cooling air on their faces as the fiery ball slowly disappeared over the tree tops, taking its heat to another part of the world.

Jill looked across the field to where the lonely ewe stood tethered. As if suddenly aware of Jill's attention, the unhappy animal gave a series of shrill bleats. She was isolated from the rest of the flock and desperately afraid. She had never before been alone, from birth to the present, there had always been familiar woolly backs grazing around her, always answering bleats to her cry. But now she had suddenly been dragged away from her companions, and tied up in a strange and lonely place, a place where no soft bleats answered her distress calls. She bent her head to crop the grass, but was uneasy. Every few moments she looked around, sensing danger.

Brian saw the direction of Jill's gaze and voiced her feelings. "I hope they do for the sake of that poor old girl out there."

Sentiment was not Broadwood's strong point. "Why? It doesn't know what's in store for it. It's got a whole field to itself. I bet it's never had it so good." Jill didn't laugh.

"The condemned ram ate a hearty breakfast," she murmured.

Morrison looked at his watch. "Good job the RSPCA haven't got wind of this little caper. Well, isn't it about time we got under cover?"

Broadwood nodded. "Yes. Although I doubt if anything will happen for a few hours yet."

"If it happens at all," added Brian quietly.

The van was partially concealed by trees and bushes. Morrison and Broadwood were both carrying rifles as a precaution against the cat sensing their presence and choosing an alternative supper to the one officially on the menu. There was a sense of unreality about the whole scene. As they climbed back into the cramped van, both Jill and Brian were conscious that they were in an isolated moorland area of Devon, surrounded by hidden snipers, waiting for a man-killer to make its appearance. The last glow from the dying sun streaked the sky with gold and crimson bands, against which the forest trees stood tall and black. A pheasant winged its way across the clearing, the gold of its feathers glinting in the sunset, the light changing the whole bird to molten copper. In a treetop, a blackbird trilled its last warning for others to keep off its territory before tucking its head under its ruffled feathers and settling down to sleep. From the darkness of the forest an owl hooted. The day shift was ending and the night shift was coming on duty.

Despite the warm evening air, Jill shivered. She felt afraid, even in the security of the van.

Broadwood was making radio contact, talking to each position in turn, checking that his men were alert and ready. "It'll probably be a long night." he told them. "Nothing might happen but don't drop your guard. Remember this is no nice little pussycat, it's already killed. Don't relax and add to the menu. Each unit report on the hour, every hour. Just give your number, no more. If your voices carry they will alert the beast, and at best, blow the stake, at worse, provide it with an army supper."

To hear the warning given by the sergeant major to his experienced men only served to increase the tension for the others.

"It can't get your men, can it?" asked Brian.

Broadwood pursed his lips. "This beast is cunning, faster than anything I've come across, and built to be a perfectly designed killing machine. It also may have developed a taste for human flesh and having already attacked and killed, it won't be in awe of us. It will actually think it's superior. Remember, just as it can scent and hear the ewe, it can also detect our presence. Still, each position is overlooked by the next, so not only are two men watching for themselves, they are also covering the next pair. If anything moves out there, they'll see it. Have you ever seen an image intensifier?"

"No," said Jill, still believing they should cancel the whole operation.

The sergeant major patted the bulky sight on his rifle. "Even in the dark, providing there's some starlight, these sights mean we can see quite clearly." He slipped the ammunition pack out and handed her the rifle. "Look through that out of the window and you'll see the effect."

Jill took hold of the weapon and lifted it with difficulty. She was amazed by the weight of it. Pointing it out of the window into the deepening gloom, she looked through the eyepiece. The effect was astonishing. The whole scene was suddenly transformed into a vivid lime green desert, the light was quite harsh, the sky, ground and trees all glowing with an eerie green light.

"It's weird," said Jill, handing the rifle to Brian so that he could see the effect.

"That's amazing!" he said, "That green light is quite a strain on the eyes."

The sergeant major took back his weapon. "We train snipers to keep the sights at the ready but to use their own eyesight until they suspect movement. Then a quick glance through the sight will confirm or eliminate whatever they've spotted. Usually a bird or a branch moving in the wind, but if a sniper is in position against them, the sight gives a clear view of the target." He slipped the ammunition pack back into position on the gun. "Now I suggest we keep talking to a minimum."

They settled down for a long wait and watched as dusk became night. Ahead of them in the darkness the poor ewe bleated plaintively, the sound being punctuated by the occasional screech of an owl. The two professionals sat motionless as the hours passed slowly while the amateurs of the team suffered agonies. Brian developed cramp in one of his legs, then the offending limb decided to go to sleep, to awaken an hour or so later with appalling 'pins and needles'. He wriggled his toes to alleviate the pain, but the sharp stabs just increased with every movement.

At the same time, Brian's suffering was nothing compared to the problems faced by Jill as she began to notice the existence of her bladder. Soon her whole concentration was given over to the urgent problem of emptying it. General discomfort gave way to the pain, and that in turn changed to agony. She bit her lip and tried not to wriggle.

"Oh, if only I'd not had that last cup of coffee," she thought desperately, trying mind over matter. 'I do not want the loo. I do not want the loo. I do not want.....'

But she did, and there was nothing she could do about it until daylight. Apart from the fact she might alert the cat by slipping out of the van, or even be attacked, those possibilities were not the main deterrent. It was the thought that if she did slip out to crouch in the bushes, she would be illuminated in a lime green desert to a circle of intently watching snipers.

At about four in the morning they were suddenly alerted by the increased volume of wails from the tethered ewe. The sky was a clear star-spangled night and they could see the white shape of the animal beginning to pull and kick at her rope.

"Is something happening?" whispered Jill, her personal problems momentarily forgotten.

"Quiet," Broadwood breathed. "The ewe senses danger. Could just be a fox, but whatever it is, she's spooked."

The ewe increased her wailing, the terror in her cries reminding Jill of a frightened child calling for its mother after a nightmare. She longed to rescue the poor creature, but it was too late. The ewe's fate was sealed. Brian sensed her feelings and patted her hand.

"It will be all right," he whispered in her ear, ignoring Broadwood's disapproving glance at the breaking of silence. "They will get the cat first." He sounded more confident than he actually felt.

On the edge of the forest the cat crouched low in the undergrowth, scenting the air uneasily. There was something wrong, the man smell was too strong and all around her. This was not the pattern she was accustomed to. Usually the man smell was isolated, one or two of the man animals together, seldom more. The only times she smelt the man-scent so strongly, she had felt in danger from them. She settled down, her tail lashing from side to side, and waited. She was hungry. She had eaten well off the man animals but that had been a few days before; she was now ready to feast again and the scent in the air proclaimed an ample supply of food. At the same time, instinct warned her against any hasty move. She remembered the loud noises that hurt. The memory caused the cat to turn and lick her twisted hind leg, her legacy from her encounter with Trapper.

The terrified ewe struggled against the tether, she knew the predator was close and her instinct was to run, to seek safety within the flock. Yet however hard she fought to free herself from the rope restraining her, the ewe couldn't escape. Finally exhausted, she collapsed, choking in the tangled rope, lying panting, her legs twitching, her eyes rolling from side to side, waiting for the attack she was sure was coming.

The cat was undecided. The ewe looked inviting, alone and apparently crippled, unable to run, but the man scent was strong and the pull of the sweet fleece-less prey undeniable. The cat made up her mind and slowly started to edge forward, belly crawling through the undergrowth. The ewe, detecting the movement, bleated frantically.

In the van the radio suddenly crackled into life.

"Position five reporting. Movement at twelve o' clock," a voice whispered.

Broadwood scanned the area through his night sight. "Got it!" he murmured, then spoke softly into the radio. "All units. Confirmed movement at twelve o' clock of position five, Looks like our baby. Over. "

All eyes strained into the darkness until shadows became solids and solids shadows. Every bush, every clump of grass became suspect. Broadwood touched Morrison's arm and gestured, passing him the night sights.

"Position two, looks like you're on the menu," whispered Broadwood calmly. "The cat is moving towards you at three o' clock. It appears to be stalking you." Jill clung to Brian's arm and stared out into the darkness. She could see nothing, but she was acutely aware of the two men lying vulnerable and unprotected out in the open.

"Oh dear God! Please let them be safe!"

After such a long time waiting, everything suddenly happened at once. The cat having chosen its target, it slithered and wriggled to within striking distance, then it bunched itself, tail lashing, and prepared to spring. With a warning snarl it launched itself across the open ground towards its prey with tremendous speed. At once, all hell was let loose. From all points around the clearing came flashes of light and loud explosions as the snipers concentrated their firepower into the centre. The cat realised its danger too late and tried to change course, twisting its body in mid-air but the firepower was too heavy and bullets tore into the writhing flesh. The animal screamed and lashed out, trying to fight off its attackers, but it could see nothing, only feel the red hot pain as whatever it was, struck again and again. It rolled over with a terrible high-pitched screech, biting at the air, its claws unsheathed as its front paws boxed at nothing. Then, with a supreme effort, it leapt towards the trees, to darkness and safety. Bullets whistled after it, smashing into the conifers, exploding branches into splinters.

"Cease firing and hold your positions," bellowed Broadwood over the radio. "We've got it!"

A roar across from the surrounding countryside as the soldiers cheered. The tension was over, and only the poor ewe continued shaking with fright. By some miracle, the animal had been missed by the flying bullets but the combination of the proximity of the cat and the sudden gunfire had reduced the terrified creature to a nervous wreck. Jill flung her arms around Brian's neck. "It's all over!" She was crying. He held her tightly.

"Thank God," he murmured.

"Amen to that," said Broadwood cheerfully, slapping Brian on the back.

They raced out of the van, running towards the area of the kill.

"Bring out the search lights," shouted Broadwood, his moment of elation gone. Once more he was a professional performing a professional task. "It can't have run far, not with that amount of lead in it. As soon as we're ready we'll move in to make sure it's dead."

It was dawn before they found the mangled cat almost a quarter of a mile from the spot where it had been hit. They approached the bloody remains with caution, but it was quite dead. When examined, it was found to have been hit eleven times. Jill dropped to her knees beside the carcass.

"Look at this. It's been shot before and the hind leg has knitted badly." She pointed to the twisted shrivelled back leg. "That's obviously why it turned killer. Some bastard shot the creature and left it badly injured." She stroked the bloody limp head, wiping away the flecks of pink stained foam from the muzzle. "You poor old girl, it wasn't your fault, was it?"

Broadwood kicked the carcass with his foot. He didn't feel any sentimental sympathy for the animal.

"Is it a leopard?" asked Brian.

"It's certainly leopard size…" began Morrison before Jill interrupted.

"But it looks a bit odd. It could be a hybrid. Most of the big cats are genetically close and can interbreed between species," said Jill, studying the head.

"Well, whatever it is, it's dead," said Broadwood briskly. "Our job is finished."

Jill looked at Brian. "It is really all over now, isn't it?" He put his arms around her shoulders and hugged her.

"Yes, love, it's over."

* * *

A black unmarked helicopter appeared in the dawn sky within half an hour of the confirmed kill and Broadwood and his men were flown out of the area. The sergeant major had shaken hands with Brian, Jill and Morrison.

"Nice to work with you folks. Take care."

Then he was gone, as if he had never been there.

A blackbird sang lustily from a nearby branch. In the clearing the ewe finally accepted the existence of the tether and began to graze peacefully, the terror of the former night forgotten. The cat's body was manhandled into the back of a police Landrover for disposal. As the vehicle bumped over the rough ground, the head swung, the once bright eyes filming over with the blind blue sheen of death.

It was over.

In the excitement of the moment, no one gave any thought to their earlier suspicions of a second cat or the possibility of cubs.

The black cat had been the killer.

The black cat was dead.

CHAPTER 12

The sound of the shots echoed across the forestry plantation, waking the sleeping cubs with a start. The male lifted its head and spat in the direction of the sound, attempting to challenge whatever had disturbed them, but the more timid female shrank back, frightened.

Although only a few months old, they were big strong cubs, for despite their mother's disability, she had fed them well.

Other sounds filled the forest, shouts and bangs, confusing them as they huddled together, frightened by the noise, instinctively crouching low in the comfortable fork of the tree. They sensed danger was close, their unease confirmed by the terrifying high-pitched screams that followed. Screams they knew to be their mother's. Then the screams cut off suddenly. To the cubs, the silence was more terrible than their mother's cries. They burrowed into the shelter of the branches and waited for her to return.

All around them, they heard other sounds, unfamiliar noises that did not belong to their forest world. They wanted their mother, whimpering softly, calling her. Eventually the disturbance ceased, and everything went quite. The other creatures of the forest began to relax. A vixen yipped from the hillside and an owl flapped lazily across the clearing, disturbing a sleeping woodpigeon that crashed, panic-stricken, through the branches. The cubs listened; they were hungry. They watched from their high perch and waited patiently. A scent drifted on the cool night breeze. It was a scent the cubs recognised. They lifted their heads and sniffed the air. They could smell their mother and they could smell blood. There were other unfamiliar scents, and despite her scent being so near, their mother did not come. They could also smell the bitter stench of terror, a combination of sweat and urine, and they knew that something was terribly wrong. They lay quiet, watching with unblinking golden eyes as the moon rose high in the sky, waiting. Dawn light filtered through the branches before they finally slept.

That evening they awoke to feel real hunger for the first time in their young lives, an empty gnawing pain that couldn't be ignored. They could still smell the scent of blood mingled with the smell of their mother on the night breeze, but it was growing fainter. They made high-pitched chittering noises, calling for her, needing her familiar presence and her protection - needing to be fed. Still she did not come. They knew they must remain hidden, knew they should not leave the place where she had left them.

For two days they waited, sleeping part of the time, but when awake, mewing faintly, whimpering their distress. By the third night, they were hungry and thirsty, desperately longing for the rough loving caress of their mother's tongue, the soft milky warmth of her belly, the reassurance of her presence.

Finally, weak with hunger, they slithered and slid down the tree trunk to go in search of her. Like all young abandoned animals, they had to learn quickly, or die. They learnt. Although the instinct to hunt was powerful and they had been taught the basics of survival by their mother, their first clumsy attempts to catch a prey were doomed to failure. They were noisy and slow but, driven by hunger, they became fast learners.

Their first kill was a roosting pheasant, which they encountered by accident. The bird was hunched, a ball of golden feathers, its head tucked under its wing, perched high in a tree and sleeping soundly, believing itself secure from passing predators. No fox could reach it and the surrounding foliage provided protection from birds of prey. Its instinct, however, had not prepared it for a pair of fierce, hungry, tree climbing predators. The cubs pounced together, almost losing their prize by getting their legs entangled while the shocked pheasant, screeching loudly, tried to break free in a shower of feathers. The unfortunate bird failed in its escape bid.

At first the cubs in their eagerness, found it difficult to find the flesh under the blanket of down and feather. They choked and coughed as they ripped the warm carcass apart, made frantic by the scent and taste of the hot blood that spurted over them. One bird was not enough to still the pangs of hunger, but it provided enough energy to find further food. Although so young, they were large enough to protect themselves from the other predators that roamed the woods. Ground-bound foxes and badges were no match for the arboreal cats. They survived on a diet of small mammals and birds, catching mice and voles, crunchy mouthfuls that bounced through the undergrowth. Even scurrying beetles were eaten – anything that could represent food was chased and devoured with enthusiasm.

After they had first left the security of the tree, the cubs discovered an area of ground that smelt strongly of their mother. Her scent was everywhere, but so was the smell of blood and death. Somehow they understood the terrible truth. Just as they killed and fed on the tiny creatures around them, something had killed and eaten their mother. For the first few days they continued to call for her, but the calling grew less frequent as the days passed and they learnt to be independent.

As the weeks passed, they grew rapidly, becoming skilled hunters and finding larger prey such as hares and rabbits. In time their mother became nothing more than a distant memory of warm milky comfort and the touch of a rough tongue.

They hunted and played together like domestic kittens, scuttling up the tree trunks, swinging from the lower limbs, hanging by their front paws, their bodies dangling like black furry fruits from the swaying branches.

As they grew older and stronger, their play became serious rehearsals for adult life. They boxed and fought, standing on their hind legs, striking at one another with claw-sheathed paws, or rolling in the pine needles, kicking with a disembowelling movement.

Growing fast, they soon discovered the joys of chasing the deer.

Working as a team, they harried and worried the slender fleet-footed animals, but were still too small to make a kill. Even the deer understood that it was only a matter of time.

The winter was hard for them. Prey was scarce and they often went hungry. When they did kill, there was seldom enough meat to satisfy them both. The female suffered most, always denied first access to the prey by her stronger sibling. She would have died during the bitterly cold weather if it had not been for the constant supply of carrion. Other animals also fared badly in the harsh conditions of the winter months, especially the herbivores. The very old and the very young found it hard to survive on the nibbled conifer shoots and bark of trees. The weak collapsed and once down, were an easy prey for all carnivores.

Humans stayed away from the moors in the winter, preferring to stay within the warm confines of their homes, so the cubs did not come up against the only animal that represented a danger to them. Not even the foresters or deer wardens suspected the existence of the two cubs.

The big cat was dead, but two were quietly waiting to take her place.

* * *

It was spring. The forest was shedding its dead mantle and fresh growth was pushing through the rotting carpet of the previous year's leaves. Primroses were scattered in creamy clumps along the earthy banks and the undergrowth was filled with scurrying creatures, all intent on making burrows and nests suitable for the rearing of their young.

The brown male cat also felt the mating urge. He had not heard the female call, but he knew it was time for their coupling. He trod the familiar paths of her territory in anticipation, glad to be away from the high tors where he had spent the winter.

He stood motionless and sniffed the air, searching for his mate's scent. He snarled as he picked up the pungent odour of the cubs, warning them to keep out of his way. Although they were his offspring, he had no sense of loyalty towards them. The female was too young to interest him, the male too small to be a challenge. For now they were safe because of their youth.

He padded along a deer path, frustrated by his lack of success in tracing his mate. There was nothing of her on the wind, not even her normal smell. He was hungry, having travelled some miles to join her, and his thoughts turned from mating to feeding.

A new scent came wafting towards him. It was familiar and his mouth watered. The female had introduced him to the delicacy, and now that he was back in her territory, he recognised the smell of the prey.

High in the tree canopy, the cubs lay quietly waiting for the male to pass. They did not know the brown cat as their father, they had no memory of him and were only aware that he represented danger.

Instinctively they understood that they should keep out of his way. The young cats settled down in the fork of the tree and remained motionless, only their bright eyes revealing they were awake.

A large crossbreed dog bounded along the woodland path, ahead of his owner, a middle-aged woman wearing a waxed jacket and green wellington boots. She strode purposefully along the muddy track, swinging a stout walking stick, breathing in the damp earthy smell of the forest, glad to be out of the town with its polluted air and noisy traffic. She was a widow, the dog her constant companion since she had retired to Devon after her husband's death. Not wealthy but comfortably off, she loved the country life and enjoyed long walks with her dog. She was thinking about the hot buttered crumpets and fresh ground coffee waiting in her cosy kitchen.

She never reached home. The alarm was sounded when a warden noticed the car parked at the roadside three days running. A police check confirmed the owner and a neighbourhood check revealed that she had not been seen for a few days. Milk stood on her doorstep and letters lay on the mat.

A search was organised in the locality of the parked car, the suspicion being that Mrs Green had met with an accident somewhere on the moors. This suspicion was strengthened when searchers found her dog, cowering and terrified, wandering loose.

Inspector Brough was unhappy at another person going missing on his patch. Runaways were commonplace: all districts had them. Brough felt he was having more than his fair share of disappearances. Despite his irritation, he did not suspect a repeat of the horrors of the year before. Mrs Green was simply an unfortunate hillwalker who had probably suffered an accident.

He couldn't believe the news when he took the call from one of the shocked search leaders.

"The body's where?"

Twenty minutes later he stood in the woodland glade, staring in horror at the sight of what remained of a half eaten body wedged in the fork of a large tree.

"Oh, shit" he exclaimed. "Not again…"

*

Brian Henderson could scarcely believe the news when he took the call at the office." You're joking," he told George Wells. "We killed the bloody thing."

"Maybe," commented George quietly. "But a lady walking her dog has ended up half eaten and stuck up a tree, just like Drew."

"Oh, my God!" Brian felt his legs go weak and remembered the terrifying chase through the wood to Mrs Briant's house. "It can't be back. We shot the creature."

"Did we shoot the wrong one?" suggested George. "We did suspect there were two."

It was a question that everyone concerned was asking, but no one could answer, not even Broadwood when he arrived to discuss the tragic new developments with the senior ranking police officers. He came in civvie clothing to avoid attracting attention, although it was hard to miss a man of his size, whatever he was wearing. He sat on the corner of Brough's desk, his face serious.

"Both the vet and Morrison said they felt the cat had had young that year, although we never confirmed it by any sightings. The general opinion was that any cubs would be too young to survive without their mother. If she had bred and a cub survived, could it be responsible for this latest killing?"

Brough shook his head. "I had a word with Morrison on the 'phone. He said definitely not. Cubs were unlikely to survive without their mother, but if they had, they would not be capable of eating the amount of meat missing from the victim, nor of lugging her up the tree. They simply wouldn't be big enough. According to Morrison, this latest kill is either by the same cat as last year, or else another full-sized feline."

Broadwood grimaced. "Great. That's all we need. Another bloody killer roaming the countryside."

His opinion was shared by everyone who had been involved in the previous year's hunt. Brian discussed his former suspicions with the sergeant- major when they met up later in the day at Jill's cottage.

"You thought there might be two animals out there," said Broadwood thoughtfully. "Could the other one be the killer?"

"I wasn't sure if there were two, it was just that some of the sightings seemed to be of a different coloured cat, explained Brian."It seemed important in the beginning, but later, well, I just put it down to a trick of light."

"But it might not have been?"

"No, Jill said a brown one could only be a puma, which was unlikely to attack humans."

"Not impossible, though," muttered the sergeant-major, "And something shoved the lady up a tree."

The hunt was on again.

* * *

It was decided to use the same people and methods that had succeeded in the previous year. The only member of the original team unable to take part was Morrison, as he was away on a project studying tigers in Siberia.

Speed was important. If the second cat was a male, expert advice was that there was no certainty it would remain in the area for any length of time. The fear was that the cat would search for the female and, failing to find her, pass on to another territory. Once it left the known site, it could turn up anywhere across the mainland. The danger to public safety was serious, a big cat could kill every three or four days. If the big cat kept on the move, no one was safe in the British countryside.

Consulted over the 'phone, Morrison suggested they had only days, perhaps hours, before the second cat would move on. They could already be too late.

Within twenty-four hours, Broadwood once more had his men in position and the surrounding moorland was clear of sheep. Local gamekeepers and police officers were going to make the sweep through the forestry, with the professional soldiers waiting on the outskirts of the trees. Broadwood was not risking a repeat of the first hunt; this time the snipers would be waiting.

The beaters set off in a single line almost shoulder to shoulder. They worked in pairs, one staring ahead at ground level, the other concentrating overhead. No one fancied the idea of a killer cat landing on them from above. They moved forward slowly and noisily, every one tense, straining to listen for the slightest rustle ahead. The sergeant major was controlling the hunt from the operation centre, keeping in touch with all groups via the radio. Working with the line of beaters, Brian missed the security of the big man's presence as the row of grim faced men moved slowly through the flickering shadows of the creaking branches overhead.

The first three sweeps were negative, only deer and foxes driven out into the open. The hunt went on. As the beaters grew weary, they were relieved by others. On the map in the mobile head quarters, each block of land was marked on the grid and eliminated as it was cleared. The searchers moved on.

On the fourth sweep, everyone was beginning to despair. Were they already too late? Was the cat miles away, hunting a new territory?

The cubs crouched low in the high branches and listened to the strange sounds in the forest. The scent of so many humans and the loud noise reminded them of something.

wakened a distant memory of when they were very young. They no longer thought of their mother, but they associated the scents and sounds with a terrifying event in their lives.

They remained silent and watched with bright golden eyes, waiting.

It was a gamekeeper who detected the first rustle ahead of him. He spoke quickly into his radio and blew a whistle. At once the beaters stopped, everyone straining in the silence, attempting to hear any sound ahead of the line. A large animal was moving away from them. There was no crashing of panic, just a rhythmic crack of lower branches as something steadily pushed its way through the undergrowth. The beaters were instantly alert, tired legs and aching backs forgotten. Even the police officers knew that it wasn't a deer or fox that was moving ahead of them.

Broadwood alerted the snipers of the direction of the sounds. Everyone waited, tense and expectant.

The cat moved stealthily through the trees, his nostrils wrinkling at the strong scent. There was prey in the forest, but the smell was too strong; it was all around him. He was confused and anxious. Taking avoiding action, the cat sprang up into the large oak, his claws biting into the corky bark as he scrabbled up into the shelter of the canopy. He settled comfortably on a large branch, his paws tucked neatly under him, and was lost to view in the shadows. The man-scent grew overwhelming. The cat licked his lips, almost tasting the sweet flesh.

A gamekeeper edged forward. The line was moving very slowly now, all eyes and ears were alert, each man trying to detect any movement ahead. Again the beaters were signalled to stop. The gamekeeper froze. The forest was menacingly silent; even birdsong was noticeably absent. The big cat curled his lip with a faint hiss, revealing his curved creamy white canines. His pink tongue lapped across the lethal ivory. He could no longer resist the lure of the unsuspecting prey.

He bunched his muscles for the spring. At the last moment, the man heard the rustle and looked up, just as the cat dropped like a stone from the cover of the tree.

The man screamed.

It was all over very quickly. As the terrifying cry echoed through the trees, a loud roar of human sound filled the air. The cat broke out of cover and bounded across the open moorland. The moment it was within range, a hail of bullets were focused in its direction, the ground around it erupting in spurts of soil. The cat twisted and screamed before rolling over on the turf, biting and snarling at its unseen attacker. The gunfire continued and the cat jerked spasmodically then lay still, the blood steaming as it flowed across the torn carcass to form puddles on the short grass.

The snipers gave a roar of triumph that was heard echoing through the trees to the waiting line of beaters.

"They got the bastard!" one man shouted, and the beaters yelled their approval and congratulations. For the first time that day, the hunters relaxed.

Everyone, civilian and military, rushed towards the twitching body of the animal, eager at last to face their quarry.

No one noticed the missing man as he staggered out of the trees, one hand covering his mutilated face, blood spurting from a severed artery, the other still holding his unfired gun. Ahead he could see his companions and neighbours. He opened his mouth, calling for help, yet he could hear no sound. His throat was constricted with terror, the scream was silent. He stumbled on towards the other men who were gathered around the steaming corpse of the cat.

"Help me."

His voice was faint and high-pitched, the sound whirling away on the moorland breeze, blending with the distant cry of the buzzard and screech of the curlew.

Only Broadwood's keen hearing picked up the sound.

With a shout he raced across to the fallen man, yelling for the medics.

The victim had dropped to his knees, his eyes wide with horror as he gazed towards the running figures. Broadwood reached him first, the sergeant major's long legs pounding over the uneven ground. The injured man's expression was one of puzzlement. Unable to comprehend the situation, he stared up in mute pleading, the torn flesh of his face hanging in a flap, his cheek sliced from just below the eye to the jaw-line by four parallel gouges that continued in bloody rips across the shoulder of his shredded jacket.

The man toppled over, the surrounding grass blades splattered with red.

A hush fell on the onlookers as the cheering men were silenced by the spectacle.

By the time the injured gamekeeper was receiving medical attention, the snipers had already packed up and were moving out. A black Chinook helicopter, its blades whirring with a rush of wind, lifted off as the last of the men leapt aboard. They did not wait to discover the fate of the casualty. For them it was a job completed.

Only Broadwood remained to attend the debriefing. He looked down at the bloody remains of the dead cat. Jill knelt beside the carcass.

"Poor beast," she murmured.

"Is it a puma?" the sergeant-major asked. They both stared at the golden brown blood-streaked fur. Jill nodded.

"The head is rather mangled, but by the colour, I'd say it is a mature male puma."

"You realise what this means," said Brian in a low voice. "The two cats may have produced cubs and those might have been young cat prints we saw in the forest. And if this cat was dad, we haven't heard the last of big cats on the moors." He looked across at Brough who had just joined them.

"Maybe," murmured the police officer, "but there is no way I can sanction another hunt based on guesswork." He stared down at the mutilated corpse. "No one has reported seeing cubs and we have no firm evidence any exist. Anyway Dartmoor is a huge area."

Jill gazed around them towards the distant hills and forested valleys. "Morrison believed they wouldn't have survived." She paused. "But if he is wrong and their mother fed them human flesh, in less than a year they will be fully mature and..." she didn't finish the sentence.

"In which case," said Brian, "the authorities had better start putting up warning notices for hikers right now before the summer rush starts."

"No way," said Brough abruptly. "You cannot start a panic based on mere speculation. Anyway we could hunt for weeks and never find them so we could not offer the public any protection. No. We must keep the suspicion strictly to ourselves and just hope that if they did exist, they have not survived the death of their mother."

* * *

In the forest the young cats remained high in the branches of their favourite tree until the man scent had faded. The moon rose high in the sky, a huge pale disc, touching the tips of the firs with silver. An owl hooted nearby and a young buck moved cautiously along the forest track. It was time for the pair to go hunting. They leapt down to land on the thick carpet of pine needles with a soft thud. The male snarled silently, his sister crouching low, deferring to his superiority, her ears laid back, her lip curled.

The cubs were a year old.

Already the deer were no longer safe.

APPENDIX

The following reports are not fictitious; they are extracts taken from just a few of the hundreds of newspaper articles concerning big cat sightings throughout the British Isles that have been published over the past twenty years:

ARMED POLICE HUNT PUMA

Armed police in a helicopter hunted yesterday for a puma on the loose...

...And as news of the sighting spread through the village of Stokenchurch, Bucks.

Close to the M40 motorway, anxious parents hurried their children indoors.

News of the World, 17th April 1983

MARINES QUIT PUMA HUNT

Royal Marines yesterday called off their hunt for the Beast of Exmoor, a dangerous animal believed to be a puma. The animal has killed 80 sheep and lambs on the North Devon Moors....

...During the week the Marines spotted a "black and powerful animal" but couldn't get a shot in....

Sunday Express, 30th May 1983.

PHANTOM KILLER OF THE MOORS MYSTERY STILL UNSOLVED

Hundreds of armed farmers, co-ordinated by the police, have scoured the fields and woods; helicopters have overflown the dragnet, acting as spotting posts; the support of local hunts has been enlisted, ...

North Devon Journal, 28th July 1983

BLACK BEAST ALERT AFTER VIDEO SHOTS

People on the outskirts of Exeter have been put on alert after "spy in the sky" cameras revealed panther-like beasts on the prowl near woodlands... The black sleeky animals, the size of Alsatians, have been seen by staff working on an electricity sub-station at Wimple...

Western Morning News, 22nd January 1988.

DON'T LET THIS BLACK CAT CROSS YOUR PATH WARN POLICE

Hikers were warned yesterday to stay away from bleak moorland as armed police combed the area for a mystery wild black panther. Officers with rifles and shotguns were called in after a farmer spotted the big cat on his land and police confirmed his sighting. "We are treating this seriously," said a police spokesman. We are warning hikers to stay away. They should take no chances."...

The hunt follows unconfirmed sightings of the animal on land above the Derbyshire town of New Mills...

Daily Express, November 1989

POLICE HUNT FOR 'PANTHER' AFTER WOMAN IS ATTACKED

Police are hunting a panther-like animal which attacked a 68-year-old woman at her home in Hayfield, Derbyshire...

...Kathleen Topliff was badly bitten on the hand when she tried to chase the animal from her dining room last Thursday. It then escaped through an open window. Inspector Rick Laithwaite, of Glossop police, said; "We have had repeated sightings but this is the first time anyone has seen it so close,"...

...Experts believe the cat is a member of the leopard family.

Independent, 3rd April 1992.

PUMA PLACED ON MOOR TO LURE MYSTERIOUS 'BEAST'

Puma from a Westcountry wildlife park was last night placed in a wooden cage on Bodmin Moor.

In a bid to lure a mysterious big cat stalking the area. Interest in obtaining clear pictorial evidence of the creature's existence and possibly capturing it has heightened following last Tuesday's early morning incident involving a 37-year-old woman from Cardinham. She told police that she was knocked unconscious by a blow to the head and came round to see just 30 feet away a large animal with a tail three feet long, crouched and moving towards her.

Western Morning News, 2nd November 1993

MARK OF THE BEAST

Shaken Sally Dyke told last night of her moment of terror when a Big Cat pounced on her and sank its claws into her side in a country churchyard...

...The panther-like creature clubbed Sally with its claws after she and her husband disturbed it as it slept among graves in Inkberrow, Worcs.

The horror attack came after she and husband Nick, 35, read about a 3ft long black cat said to have terrorised rural Worcestershire for four years... The trail led the couple to the churchyard. Ex-paratrooper Nick told how he surprised the sleeping animal...   ..."It catapulted away from me and ran towards Sally. Suddenly it performed some really peculiar acrobatics - its shoulders went one way, its hips the other and it swatted at her with its right paw. If it had clubbed her round the head it could have killed her"... Sally said..."I didn't notice the pain at first but I started bleeding quite badly. I'm sure I will be scarred for life"...

The Sun, 21st April 1994.

BODMIN WORRY OVER BIG CATS

Attacks on farm animals by big, puma-like wild cats in the West Country have prompted a top level meeting in Bodmin. NFU, Country Landowners Association, Local authority and police representatives are meeting leading MAFF officials, and local MPs. Chris Collin, Liskeard NFU group secretary, said there had been several authenticated sightings of big cats on Bodmin and other moors. He knew of one where he was certain there was one female and two cubs.

Farmers Weekly, 26th August 1994.

THERE'S BOUND TO BE A TRAGEDY SOON

PC Peter Keen, dog handler at Bodmin police station, has become an expert on Cornwall's wild big cats. He has seen pumas, with their young, three times on Bodmin Moor. One night last November, beside a forestry plantation, he surprised a puma cub in the light of his torch. Then he saw the mother approach, and hurried back to his car. "I'm nervous walking on the moor now in twilight," he confessed. "The pumas I saw were mostly dark brown in colour," he added. "I've also seen a black panther with its cub and I'm very much afraid that one day there's bound to be a tragedy."

Daily Mail, 31st December 1994.

PANTHER HUNT

Police and farmers in Hereford and Worcester are on the lookout for a large black cat that is believed to have attacked a cow. The cow survived but was left with gashes along its haunches that vets say are consistent with the type of wounds a panther would inflict...

The Times 2nd May 1995.

PREPARE FOR PATTER OF TINY PAWS

Big cats spotted on the Chase, Worcester and Cotswolds may be breeding, a University expert has warned ...But she said the only way the cats will attack human beings was if they were hurt, distressed or desperate. "If someone takes a pot shot and injures a cat, it's more likely the cat will attack or retaliate. Likewise if there are no other animals for them to hunt, they will seek humans instead"...

Burntwood Post, 11th January 1996

NEW SIGHTING OF 'BLACK BEAST'

A frightened pensioner has rekindled interest in a mysterious black beast said to be roaming the Gloucestershire countryside. The woman, aged 62, spotted a giant cat-like creature from her bedroom window in Churchill Grove, Tewkesbury, in the early hours of Wednesday... She told police the animal emerged from the bushes, sniffed the air then disappeared into the darkness...

...Inspector Dean Walker of Gloucestershire police said the woman, who does not wish to be named, often gets up in the middle of the night to watch foxes because she cannot sleep...

Western Daily Press, 10th January 1997.

PUMA TERROR

Police yesterday launched an investigation after a woman told officers that her 10 stone rottweiler fought off a 4ft puma-like beast which pounced in woodland in Warwickshire...

Press and Journal, 13th February. 1998.

POSTSCRIPT

Let all who carry guns in the British countryside take heed. Animals that develop a taste for human flesh are usually disabled or too old to hunt their natural prey. A healthy big cat can easily survive in the British countryside without posing a danger to human neighbours. But an injured big cat is a very dangerous big cat.

Di Francis, 2012

THE WORLD'S WEIRDEST PUBLISHING COMPANY

HOW TO START A PUBLISHING EMPIRE

Unlike most mainstream publishers, we have a non-commercial remit, and our mission statement claims that "we publish books because they deserve to be published, not because we think that we can make money out of them". Our motto is the Latin Tag *Pro bona causa facimus* (we do it for good reason), a slogan taken from a children's book *The Case of the Silver Egg* by the late Desmond Skirrow.

WIKIPEDIA: "The first book published was in 1988. *Take this Brother may it Serve you Well* was a guide to Beatles bootlegs by Jonathan Downes. It sold quite well, but was hampered by very poor production values, being photocopied, and held together by a plastic clip binder. In 1988 A5 clip binders were hard to get hold of, so the publishers took A4 binders and cut them in half with a hacksaw. It now reaches surprisingly high prices second hand.

The production quality improved slightly over the years, and after 1999 all the books produced were ringbound with laminated colour covers. In 2004, however, they signed an agreement with Lightning Source, and all books are now produced perfect bound, with full colour covers."

Until 2010 all our books, the majority of which are/were on the subject of mystery animals and allied disciplines, were published by `CFZ Press`, the publishing arm of the Centre for Fortean Zoology (CFZ), and we urged our readers and followers to draw a discreet veil over the books that we published that were completely off topic to the CFZ.

However, in 2010 we decided that enough was enough and launched a second imprint, `Fortean Words` which aims to cover a wide range of non animal-related esoteric subjects. Other imprints will be launched as and when we feel like it, however the basic ethos of the company remains the same: Our job is to publish books and magazines that we feel are worth publishing, whether or not they are going to sell. Money is, after all - as my dear old Mama once told me - a rather vulgar subject, and she would be rolling in her grave if she thought that her eldest son was somehow in `trade`.

Luckily, so far our tastes have turned out not to be that rarified after all, and we have sold far more books than anyone ever thought that we would, so there is a moral in there somewhere…

Jon Downes,
Woolsery, North Devon
July 2010

Other Books in Print

Sea Serpent Carcasses - Scotland from the Stronsa Monster to Loch Ness by Glen Vaudrey
The CFZ Yearbook 2012 edited by Jonathan and Corinna Downes
ORANG PENDEK: Sumatra's Forgotten Ape by Richard Freeman
THE MYSTERY ANIMALS OF THE BRITISH ISLES: London by Neil Arnold
CFZ EXPEDITION REPORT: India 2010 by Richard Freeman *et al*
The Cryptid Creatures of Florida by Scott Marlow
Dead of Night by Lee Walker
The Mystery Animals of the British Isles: The Northern Isles by Glen Vaudrey
THE MYSTERY ANIMALS OF THE BRTISH ISLES: Gloucestershire and Worcestershire by
Paul Williams
When Bigfoot Attacks by Michael Newton
Weird Waters – The Mystery Animals of Scandinavia: Lake and Sea Monsters by Lars Thomas
The Inhumanoids by Barton Nunnelly
Monstrum! A Wizard's Tale by Tony "Doc" Shiels
CFZ Yearbook 2011 edited by Jonathan Downes
Karl Shuker's Alien Zoo by Shuker, Dr Karl P.N
Tetrapod Zoology Book One by Naish, Dr Darren
The Mystery Animals of Ireland by Gary Cunningham and Ronan Coghlan
Monsters of Texas by Gerhard, Ken
The Great Yokai Encyclopaedia by Freeman, Richard
NEW HORIZONS: Animals & Men issues 16-20 Collected Editions Vol. 4
by Downes, Jonathan
A Daintree Diary -
Tales from Travels to the Daintree Rainforest in tropical north Queensland, Australia
by Portman, Carl
Strangely Strange but Oddly Normal by Roberts, Andy
Centre for Fortean Zoology Yearbook 2010 by Downes, Jonathan
Predator Deathmatch by Molloy, Nick
Star Steeds and other Dreams by Shuker, Karl
CHINA: A Yellow Peril? by Muirhead, Richard
Mystery Animals of the British Isles: The Western Isles by Vaudrey, Glen

Giant Snakes - Unravelling the coils of mystery by Newton, Michael
Mystery Animals of the British Isles: Kent by Arnold, Neil
Centre for Fortean Zoology Yearbook 2009 by Downes, Jonathan
CFZ EXPEDITION REPORT: Russia 2008 by Richard Freeman *et al*, Shuker, Karl (fwd)
Dinosaurs and other Prehistoric Animals on Stamps - A Worldwide catalogue
by Shuker, Karl P. N
Dr Shuker's Casebook by Shuker, Karl P.N
The Island of Paradise - chupacabra UFO crash retrievals,
and accelerated evolution on the island of Puerto Rico by Downes, Jonathan
The Mystery Animals of the British Isles: Northumberland and Tyneside by Hallowell, Michael J
Centre for Fortean Zoology Yearbook 1997 by Downes, Jonathan (Ed)
Centre for Fortean Zoology Yearbook 2002 by Downes, Jonathan (Ed)
Centre for Fortean Zoology Yearbook 2000/1 by Downes, Jonathan (Ed)
Centre for Fortean Zoology Yearbook 1998 by Downes, Jonathan (Ed)
Centre for Fortean Zoology Yearbook 2003 by Downes, Jonathan (Ed)
In the wake of Bernard Heuvelmans by Woodley, Michael A
CFZ EXPEDITION REPORT: Guyana 2007 by Richard Freeman *et al*, Shuker, Karl (fwd)
Centre for Fortean Zoology Yearbook 1999 by Downes, Jonathan (Ed)
Big Cats in Britain Yearbook 2008 by Fraser, Mark (Ed)
Centre for Fortean Zoology Yearbook 1996 by Downes, Jonathan (Ed)
THE CALL OF THE WILD - Animals & Men issues 11-15
Collected Editions Vol. 3 by Downes, Jonathan (ed)
Ethna's Journal by Downes, C N
Centre for Fortean Zoology Yearbook 2008 by Downes, J (Ed)
DARK DORSET -Calendar Custome by Newland, Robert J
Extraordinary Animals Revisited by Shuker, Karl
MAN-MONKEY - In Search of the British Bigfoot by Redfern, Nick
Dark Dorset Tales of Mystery, Wonder and Terror by Newland, Robert J and Mark North
Big Cats Loose in Britain by Matthews, Marcus
MONSTER! - The A-Z of Zooform Phenomena by Arnold, Neil
The Centre for Fortean Zoology 2004 Yearbook by Downes, Jonathan (Ed)
The Centre for Fortean Zoology 2007 Yearbook by Downes, Jonathan (Ed)
CAT FLAPS! Northern Mystery Cats by Roberts, Andy
Big Cats in Britain Yearbook 2007 by Fraser, Mark (Ed)
BIG BIRD! - Modern sightings of Flying Monsters by Gerhard, Ken
THE NUMBER OF THE BEAST - Animals & Men issues 6-10
Collected Editions Vol. 1 by Downes, Jonathan (Ed)
IN THE BEGINNING - Animals & Men issues 1-5 Collected Editions Vol. 1 by Downes, Jonathan
STRENGTH THROUGH KOI - They saved Hitler's Koi and other stories
by Downes, Jonathan
The Smaller Mystery Carnivores of the Westcountry by Downes, Jonathan
CFZ EXPEDITION REPORT: Gambia 2006 by Richard Freeman *et al*, Shuker, Karl (fwd)
The Owlman and Others by Jonathan Downes
The Blackdown Mystery by Downes, Jonathan

Big Cats in Britain Yearbook 2006 by Fraser, Mark (Ed)
Fragrant Harbours - Distant Rivers by Downes, John T
Only Fools and Goatsuckers by Downes, Jonathan
Monster of the Mere by Jonathan Downes
Dragons:More than a Myth by Freeman, Richard Alan
Granfer's Bible Stories by Downes, John Tweddell
Monster Hunter by Downes, Jonathan

CFZ Classics is a new venture for us. There are many seminal works that are either unavailable today, or not available with the production values which we would like to see. So, following the old adage that if you want to get something done do it yourself, this is exactly what we have done.

Desiderius Erasmus Roterodamus (b. October 18th 1466, d. July 2nd 1536) said: "When I have a little money, I buy books; and if I have any left, I buy food and clothes," and we are much the same. Only, we are in the lucky position of being able to share our books with the wider world. CFZ Classics is a conduit through which we cannot just re-issue titles which we feel still have much to offer the cryptozoological and Fortean research communities of the 21st Century, but we are adding footnotes, supplementary essays, and other material where we deem it appropriate.

Headhunters of The Amazon by Fritz W Up de Graff (1902)

Fortean Words

The Centre for Fortean Zoology has for several years led the field in Fortean publishing. CFZ Press is the only publishing company specialising in books on monsters and mystery animals. CFZ Press has published more books on this subject than any other company in history and has attracted such well known authors as Andy Roberts, Nick Redfern, Michael Newton, Dr Karl Shuker, Neil Arnold, Dr Darren Naish, Jon Downes, Ken Gerhard and Richard Freeman.

Now CFZ Press are launching a new imprint. Fortean Words is a new line of books dealing with Fortean subjects other than cryptozoology, which is - after all - the subject the CFZ are best known for. Fortean Words is being launched with a spectacular multi-volume series called *Haunted Skies* which covers British UFO sightings between 1940 and 2010. Former policeman John Hanson and his long-suffering partner Dawn Holloway have compiled a peerless library of sighting reports, many that have not been made public before.

Other books include a look at the Berwyn Mountains UFO case by renowned Fortean Andy Roberts and a series of forthcoming books by transatlantic researcher Nick Redfern. CFZ Press are dedicated to maintaining the fine quality of their works with Fortean Words. New authors tackling new subjects will always be encouraged, and we hope that our books will continue to be as ground-breaking and popular as ever.

Haunted Skies Volume One 1940-1959 by John Hanson and Dawn Holloway
Haunted Skies Volume Two 1960-1965 by John Hanson and Dawn Holloway
Haunted Skies Volume Three 1965-1967 by John Hanson and Dawn Holloway
Haunted Skies Volume Four 1968-1971 by John Hanson and Dawn Holloway
Haunted Skies Volume Five 1972-1974 by John Hanson and Dawn Holloway
Haunted Skies Volume Six 1975-1977 by John Hanson and Dawn Holloway
Grave Concerns by Kai Roberts

Police and the Paranormal by Andy Owens
Dead of Night by Lee Walker
Space Girl Dead on Spaghetti Junction - an anthology by Nick Redfern
I Fort the Lore - an anthology by Paul Screeton
UFO Down - the Berwyn Mountains UFO Crash by Andy Roberts
The Grail by Ronan Coghlan
UFO Warminster - Cradle of Contract by Kevin Goodman
Quest for the Hexham Heads by Paul Screeton

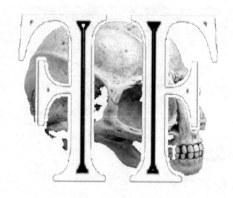

Fortean Fiction

Just before Christmas 2011, we launched our third imprint, this time dedicated to - let's see if you guessed it from the title - fictional books with a Fortean or cryptozoological theme. We have published a few fictional books in the past, but now think that because of our rising reputation as publishers of quality Forteana, that a dedicated fiction imprint was the order of the day.

We launched with four titles:

Green Unpleasant Land by Richard Freeman
Left Behind by Harriet Wadham
Dark Ness by Tabitca Cope
Snap! By Steven Bredice
Death on Dartmoor by Di Francis
Dark Wear by Tabitca Cope

Lightning Source UK Ltd.
Milton Keynes UK
UKOW03f1806160913

217317UK00010B/722/P